FOUR CORNERS MANHUNT

One Detective's Story of the 1998 Tragedy

by

Shirlee Forteneaux
and
Kathleen Quackenbush

First published by AuthorHouse 05/25/04

ISBN: 1-4184-6709-X (e-book)
ISBN: 1-4184-4246-1 (Paperback)

Library of Congress Control Number: 2004091628

This book is printed on acid free paper.

Printed in the United States of America
Bloomington, IN

ACKNOWLEDGMENTS

There are many people to thank, not only for their impressions and the information they willingly shared with us, but for their support.

We are tremendously grateful to "Matt" and "Cynthia" for trusting us to do their story —-a story that has turned out to be more fascinating and uplifting than anything we could have written about in fiction.

By entering their world, they are now a part of our lives and we will hopefully continue being their friends. We do know that the story of the Four Comers Manhunt cannot really end until the last fugitive is found. The mystery is still out there.

We also wish to give special thanks to the following people:

Christina Jameson, a close friend who originally introduced us to Matt and Cynthia and who encouraged us to write their story while helping us in any way she could.

Sally Ensign, a longtime friend who unflinchingly did the final editing on the book. She also continued giving us the encouragement we needed.

Linda Eggenberger, our "cuz" in Illinois, who willingly shared her literary knowledge with us.

To my son, Mike, who remained patient while I spent hours writing the book. To Kathleen's sons, Ryan and Jess, teenagers who told us to GO FOR IT!

To our family and friends —-you know who you are!

This book is dedicated to all the police
officers and their families whose
lives were affected on that day —

May 29, 1998

"Day by Day, what you choose, what you think, and what you do
is who you become.
Your integrity is your destiny … it is the light that guides your way."

……….. Heraclitus

PROLOGUE

MAY 29, 1998

....

Matt Nelson was in a desperate situation, and for the first time in his life, he felt he might actually die.

A heavy barrage of bullets was zipping all around him, leaving large holes in his unmarked Jeep. Being a cop, he knew guns well and had instantly recognized the sound of an automatic rifle with heavy-armored bullets.

He was crouched down beside his Jeep and could feel the heat from the bullets as they whizzed by him. *God, one head shot and it would all be over!*

Just seconds ago, he had encountered a flatbed truck barreling toward him down a narrow, county road. Slamming on his brakes, he had yanked the steering wheel to the left and skidded to a stop with the rear of his vehicle blocking the road. He had hoped to either slow down or stop the oncoming truck. However, the driver had maneuvered the truck around Matt's solitary roadblock, causing him to be without cover.

As the flatbed passed by him, he was totally exposed to a man who was leaning out of the passenger window. The guy was skinny with shoulder-length, sandy-colored hair blowing wildly across his face, and his eyes had a maniacal look to them. He was dressed in camouflage and holding an SKS automatic rifle that was aimed right at Matt's face as the truck passed within ten feet of him. The guy fired, and Matt could feel the shock of the blast as it whizzed by his shoulder, barely missing him.

What he failed to see was a second man on the flatbed of the truck who was also armed with an automatic rifle.

He rapidly cocked his shotgun and was swinging it up toward the guy hanging out of the window as the truck skidded around his car. Too late, he saw the guy in the back of the truck. A earsplitting hail of fire sounded, and he watched as his left elbow literally exploded. The impact of the bullet that found its mark felt like a heavy punch being delivered to his arm, followed by a pain comparable to what a burning hot poker must feel like.

As the searing heat from the bullet surged down his arm, he heard an unfamiliar sound and watched a fine, red mist burst out from his elbow. The shotgun fell from his hand just as a huge, gaping wound appeared where his elbow had been, and shock rushed through him.

I've been shot!

Even as that thought registered, bullets began chewing up his car again. Crouched as low as he could get beside the Jeep, he looked anxiously around for better cover. Glass was literally exploding in all directions and the noise was so loud, he felt momentarily deaf. As gunpowder thickened in the air around his face, he knew those bullets could easily go right through his vest.

Years of police training kicked in, and his brain began screaming. *COVER, COVER, COVER!* Yet his feet felt like they were cemented to the ground as the bullets slammed all around him. It sounded like bullwhips were being snapped over his head.

I gotta' move or die!

The only place he could see that might protect him was the undercarriage of his Jeep. He dived toward the back wheel of the Jeep just as a violent blow hit his right knee like a five-pound sledge hammer. He didn't let it slow him down for a minute!

Rolling under the car, he scooted beneath the driver's compartment using the left back tire and the front right tire as the only cover available to him. Bending both of his arms tightly under his chest, he tried to make himself as small a target as possible. Unknowingly he was also inhibiting the flow of blood from his left arm while in that position, which would ultimately save his life.

As he huddled there frozen in time, listening to bullets skipping under and around and into the Jeep, he closed his eyes, well aware the next shot could kill him. Had it been just an hour ago that he was about to take a bite of cake celebrating his last day as head detective for the sheriff's office?

Now shots were echoing through the San Juans, and he was alone in the battle for his life. Would he ever see his wife and son again?

ONE

....

Matt awoke to a beautiful Colorado spring morning. As he opened his eyes, he could see that the San Juan Mountains, called 'Shining Mountains' by the Ute Indians, were living up to their name today. The early sun was glistening on the last of winter snow covering the very top of the jagged peaks, causing blue-gray shadows to envelop their house.

The large bedroom window was open, and he could hear the tumbling, churning sounds of river water as it flowed and jumped over black rocks thousands of years old.

Spring this year had been wet and mild, bringing about an explosion of wildflowers on the high mountains surrounding the sprawling ranch house he and Cynthia had lovingly built for themselves two years ago.

Yeah, life was good! Matt quietly edged out of bed, stopping to look at his beautiful wife sleeping peacefully. Married just two years, he felt blessed that they had found each other at just the right time in their lives.

As he padded out into the sun-filled kitchen with its handmade wooden cabinets and ceramic bar, the cool oak floor felt good on his bare feet. Their big white Samoyed, Ranger, enthusiastically greeted him as he went to the counter to fix a pot of freshly ground coffee. Laughing softly, he rubbed the handsome dog's ear and said, "Okay, Ranger. Out you go."

As he opened the sliding glass door, Ranger bounded out into the large fenced yard and Matt knew he would soon be trying to catch the crafty gray squirrel who lived at the top of their highest pine tree; the one who would climb just far enough down the trunk to look Ranger in the eyes as he flicked his tail and scolded his dog with loud chattering sounds. It drove Ranger crazy.

Leaving Ranger to do his thing, he returned to his task of fixing the coffee before sitting down at the finely-crafted pine breakfast bar that he had made himself. Only then did he allow his thoughts to stray back to the events that had brought him to this day.

At thirty-six, he knew he was in the prime of his life, both physically and mentally. His body was lean-muscled and strong, and he had always been blessed with good health. The years of working with the Montezuma County sheriff's office had kept him sharp and in top physical condition, and he felt good about his accomplishments during that time.

He had worked his way up to the rank of Detective Sergeant and then served as lead investigator for the detective team. A short time later he had joined the sheriff's SWAT team. Only a select few make it, and Matt had qualified at the top of his class. Because he had the intelligence and character traits that made for a good cop, he was soon elected team leader.

He took the promotion seriously, knowing it meant his fellow deputies considered him to be one of their best, and they were trusting him to get them in and out of dangerous situations. That had made him feel pretty damned good, and he went out of his way to live up to their expectations.

He had always played it straight, and had no tolerance for any officer who crossed the line, like taking bribes or getting involved in drugs and other illegal activities. He was well aware that one dishonest cop can reflect on the integrity of an entire police force. The public didn't always have the best of opinions about law enforcement officers anyway; a dishonest or bullying one just made things that much worse.

When Catlin had been elected as the County's new sheriff two years ago, Matt knew instantly he wouldn't be able to interact with him in the same professional manner he had enjoyed with the former sheriff. Due to the excess baggage of political crap that often came with the job, Matt found himself at odds with the sheriff more times than he was comfortable with. It didn't take long to lose all respect for him.

Sheriff Catlin was proving daily what a mediocre leader he was, always more concerned with how each new bust would benefit him personally in the public's eye than in how the bust had occured. He didn't care if it was drugs or some kid taking a joy ride in a "borrowed" car because if someone landed in jail, he happily took credit for the arrest.

Matt remembered when Catlin won the election and became their new sheriff. He had won by a mere twenty votes. Catlin had called a staff meeting on his first day in office, and Matt attended with the expectation of hearing a prepared pep talk concerning what he planned to do to better the department. Instead, his words still rang in Matt's head. "I will start by

2

saying I expect complete loyalty from every man in this room. Anyone who has a problem with that will find themselves looking for a new job."

Their newly-elected sheriff never did address any of the issues Matt had always assumed were the most important ones such as theft, drugs or murder. The new sheriff had just one goal in mind: he wanted to be King. Matt had tried to do his job in spite of this, giving it the best he could. Three weeks ago, Sheriff Catlin had called him at home. "Matt, how's it goin'?"

Surprised by the call, Matt had replied, "Good. And you?"

Catlin had chuckled. "Real good. I called to tell you about some decisions I've made. You remember Juan Sanchez, don't you?"

"Uh, yeah. He was a Patrol Sergeant before he quit." Matt had always assumed Sanchez had quit because he and Catlin had frequently butted heads.

"Right. A damned good officer too. Anyway, I'd like you to train him. He's comin' back on board, and I've decided to promote him to head both patrol and detectives. I figure you're the best man we've got to give him the quality training he's gonna' need."

Matt was too stunned to answer. Catlin had all but promised him that same position. As he held the receiver to his ear, his throat felt dry and it became difficult to swallow.

Catlin's voice jerked him back. "Matt? You still there?"

"Yeah."

"You're probably thinkin' Juan doesn't have any detective experience, but he can learn with the right person trainin' him. Right?"

Matt's throat felt constricted. "Yeah, maybe. But there are people who can get all the training in the world, and it still won't make them a good leader." *Including you, Catlin.*

Catlin's voice turned harsh, "Is that right? Well, I believe Juan does have the right stuff, so you get the pleasure of trainin' him, startin' next week." He hung up the phone.

Matt also hung up, then sat down at the breakfast bar and stared out the window. Cynthia walked into the room at that moment and came up behind him. Putting her hands on his shoulders, she leaned down and said against his ear, "Who was that?"

He pushed out a chair next to him. "Sit down, honey."

She looked at him curiously, then sat down. "What's wrong?"

3

He shook his head. "That jerk, Catlin … he's decided to bring back a cop who quit last year. He's giving my promotion to him."

She frowned. "I don't understand."

"You'd better believe it'll benefit Catlin in some way."

She edged her chair close to him and placed her hand on his arm. "Matt, you've been unhappy with this sheriff ever since he got elected. Do you know the guy he re-hired?"

"Juan Sanchez. He was a Patrol Sergeant, but damn it, he doesn't know one thing about being a detective. You can't just walk in there and lead a team of experienced detectives. So Catlin wants me to train him for the job I was promised."

She gasped, "That's crazy! There has to be a reason behind this."

Matt felt betrayed. "All I know is that I can't stay there. I don't want to sink into that pit of nothingness I've seen other cops do. I won't do it."

"I know you won't."

He looked at Cynthia. "It's too much. I've put up with way too many things because of this guy. It's time to move on."

She had slowly nodded her head. "You could have your pick of any law enforcement agency in the state."

"I think I might apply to the Highway Patrol. Monroe has been telling me for years how much better they are to work for than the sheriff's office."

"Since Monroe's your brother, will that interfere with you getting on with them?"

"No. The big obstacle will be going through their Academy. A couple of deputies from the sheriff's office already tried to get into it, but got turned down."

"You won't have any problems qualifying."

Matt's brother had always spoken highly of the Colorado Highway Patrol's professionalism and fair attitude toward its officers. Matt knew his benefits and retirement would also be better. Frankly, his future at the sheriff's office now looked pretty bleak if he were to stay there.

The next day, he had walked into the main lobby of the sheriff's office and was bombarded by people coming up to him and asking what he thought about Sanchez getting the promotion that had been promised to him.

How the hell did they think he felt? Instead of answering them, he just shrugged his shoulders and went straight back to his office, closing the door.

He *was* curious about how his detective team would react, but when he met with them that afternoon, he was in for a big disappointment.

No one addressed it. They all acted fairly indifferent, evidently preferring to accept things however they played out. So be it. The following day, Matt contacted the Colorado Highway Patrol office in Denver and began the long process of applications and interviews in order to be accepted for the next academy.

Two weeks later, he received word that he had been accepted for the Academy and had immediately turned in his notice of resignation. No one from administration commented on his decision to quit, but they all knew why.

On the surface, most of his fellow deputies seemed to understand why he had made the determination to go over to the State Patrol. Yet as his last day approached, he began sensing twinges of jealousy, especially from those deputies who had tried out for the same academy but had been turned down.

It just cemented his decision. He was still young enough to work up the ranks again, and it had been the right time to move on with his life. In fact, he was feeling really good about the new challenges ahead of him.

The coffee pot signaled it was done, so he filled his cup with the steaming aromatic liquid and walked over to open the glass door so he could not only see the mountains, but also smell the fresh fragrance of a new day.

Birds were noisily communicating amongst themselves in the trees, and he saw how Ranger had disturbed at least three gray squirrels who were now chattering and flicking their bushy tails at him from a safe distance. Ranger was patiently standing under the tree, waiting for one of them to make a mistake and come too close. However, they never did. Matt smiled, then turned back to place his coffee cup on the breakfast bar before he sat down facing the window.

Today was his last day at work and he smiled to himself, letting the excited feeling wrap around him. He planned to pick up his son after school, as this was his weekend to have Josh. His ex-wife, Leslie, was not always on the best of terms with him, so he made it a point to never miss a scheduled weekend. Josh would be joining Cynthia and him for a planned camping trip deep into the mountains this weekend.

Cynthia would be spending the morning buying groceries and planning the menu for their outing. His wife was a great "camp cook," and he was looking forward to this time with her and his son. Finishing his coffee, he stood up and stretched, eager to begin his day. Especially *this* day.

He used the guest bathroom to shower, unwilling to wake Cynthia just yet. When he returned to their bedroom, he saw that she had already gotten up and the aroma of toast and eggs wafted on the air. Suddenly he was famished, and he hurried to finish dressing.

Following his nose to the kitchen, Matt came up behind Cynthia as she stood at the stove in her soft flannel nightgown. Wrapping his arms around her, he nudged her silky blond hair aside so he could kiss her neck and inhale the clean, unique scents that were Cynthia. "Hmm. Do you have any idea how great I feel this morning, Baby?"

She laughed and maneuvered around in his arms so she could face him. Her beautiful green eyes sparkled as they met his. "I do. And tonight we'll be sitting around a campfire counting our lucky stars. How does that sound?"

He kissed her soft lips. "Exactly like heaven."

Still feeling like he was on their honeymoon, his wife was an amazing woman and he was still in awe of how the sparks had instantly flowed between them the day they met at the sheriff's office.

* * *

Summer of 1996
....

Cynthia had been walking up the front steps of the sheriff's office and he found himself looking twice at her. Turning to a fellow deputy, he had asked, "Hey! Who's the blond?"

His buddy had laughed. "Take it easy, Matt. I hear she's not a woman to be taken lightly, and you ain't ready, son."

Matt watched as she disappeared through the door. "Yeah. You're probably right."

After his divorce three years ago, Matt had decided love was for everyone but him; that it caused loneliness and unhappiness and was usually so fleeting it just didn't make sense to get involved again. So he had been accepting relationships for whatever they offered at the moment. No one got hurt that way.

Besides, there really wasn't any reason to put his feelings out there at that time in his life. Yet deep inside, he *was* looking for something more; he just wasn't ready to acknowledge it.

When he chanced to run into Cynthia in the copy machine room a few days later, he found himself immediately drawn to the way her striking eyes seemed to sparkle as they talked. She was wearing black slacks and a green sweater that complimented her green eyes and blond hair. Her cute southern accent was a surprise, but it just added to her charms. When she left the room, he knew he was going to ask her out.

They went on their first date a week later, and he was instantly hooked. He found out she had moved to Cortez from Texas to escape an unhappy marriage; that she had been the "trophy wife" of a very wealthy man who hobnobbed with the Bushes and their family.

She confessed that she had had everything money could buy, but felt like she was the least important person in her husband's life. His whole world revolved around making money and, as he grew colder and more aloof, she became lonelier and more unhappy. One day she called a lawyer to begin divorce proceedings, packed her personal belongings and fled to Colorado where her mother lived.

Matt was a man who loved the outdoors and enjoyed camping up near the high peaks of the San Juans whenever possible. He rode a Harley Davidson motorcycle on his days off and, during the weekends, would often take his young son up into the mountains to fish and hike.

He had been pleasantly surprised when he found out the pretty high society lady from Dallas loved jumping on the back of his Harley to spend a weekend snuggled in a sleeping bag out under the stars. They would camp out at ten-thousand feet, and he found himself smiling as he thought of one weekend when an eagle had nearly knocked him off a steep cliff.

He had lost his balance trying to avoid the big bird and found himself flat on his back close to the cliff's edge. Cynthia had screamed out in fear, but once she saw he was okay, she had bent over laughing uncontrollably. That had sort of blown his rugged, mountain man image, but it was worth it to see Cynthia laugh like that.

It hadn't taken her long to fall in love with the wild and untouched parts of nature surrounding the Silverton area, and it became one of her favorite places to be. Nothing seemed to dampen her growing addiction to the high country of Colorado, something he had experienced as a young boy.

It was great to wake up to a cold, wet morning when frost had covered their tent during the night while they snuggled together in a toasty warm double sleeping bag. They would lie there listening to the noises of a nearby creek as it rushed down the steep canyon, and talk in hushed tones about their growing feelings for each other.

Later he would start a fire while Cynthia unpacked their trusty metal coffee pot. He felt he had found an unusual woman; one who believed in making camping out with him a romantic time. That had surprised and flattered him. Her culinary talents were awesome. They included fresh trout sprinkled with lemon and herbs on the grill, special baked potatoes, and for dessert, she would serve anything from caramelized bananas to grilled peaches with a unique sauce.

Candles would be lit and placed on a portable table covered with a white tablecloth while a portable tape deck would be playing soft music. A cooler was filled with ice to chill their wine. All in all, it made him feel pretty damned special.

His former wife had never really enjoyed camping much and preferred a motel to sleeping on the hard ground. Cynthia was the opposite, making everything they did together an adventure. He found himself dusting off forgotten dreams and looking forward to brand new ones.

They were married six months later and what was to have been a small, intimate wedding at a charming wedding chapel in Laughlin, Nevada, turned into a night of partying. Thirty members of his family traveled to Nevada, including his parents, his two brothers with their families, plus uncles, aunts and cousins he had not seen for years.

Two rented stretch limos carried guests to the little wedding chapel, and he had to keep pinching himself to believe it was really happening. It was also one of the happiest days of his life.

The only problem they had was with Leslie, his ex-wife. She had decided she didn't agree with his choice of a wife and was obvious in her dislike for Cynthia. Shortly before they left for the wedding, Leslie had barged into the sheriff's office and thrown his son's suitcase at Cynthia's feet. Yelling at Cynthia in front of everyone, she demanded that Josh be brought home immediately after the wedding was over. With that said, she had stomped out of the office, slamming the door behind her.

Cynthia told Matt that everyone was standing there staring at her, so she had calmly picked up Josh's suitcase and, in her best Texas drawl, had said, "I guess you just can't please everyone all the time."

Matt had laughed, liking the way she had handled it. Leslie had a habit of making it difficult for him to see Josh, and he had a feeling things would probably get worse before they got better. Leslie had remarried before he had, so he really didn't understand these continuing displays of hostility.

TWO

After breakfast, Matt prepared to leave for his last day at the sheriff's office. As he leaned down to kiss Cynthia goodbye, her face abruptly changed and he caught a look of fear in her eyes.

Pulling back in surprise, he cupped her chin in his hand and asked, "What's wrong?"

She stared at him for a long moment, then shook her head. "Nothing, honey. Just hurry up and get home." Flashing him a big smile, she kissed him. "Go on now. I'll see you later. I love you."

He hesitated, then nodded. "Me too."

At the same time Matt was leaving for his last day at work, a dispatcher from the sheriff's office put out an All Points Bulletin on a large water truck stolen from an oil field parking lot near Ignacio, Colorado.

When the three occupants of the stolen truck heard the APB on their own illegal police scanner, they began cursing. A tall, lanky man with long sandy-colored hair was sitting next to the window of the truck and exclaimed, "Damn! I thought once we got through Durango, it would be a piece of cake."

The bulky, muscular young man positioned in the middle turned to look at the driver and said, "Dan, don't go through Cortez. Use the back road that snakes around by the landfill. No one will spot us out there."

Dan nodded. "Got it."

They had almost made it into the wild canyonlands beyond the town when a police cruiser appeared behind them and Dan yelled out, "We've been made!"

All three men stared in the sideview mirrors at the cruiser, which was keeping its distance. The tall man sitting next to the window growled, "He's calling for help. Pull over."

Dan pulled the large truck over to the side of the road by a small bridge, but left the engine running. All three men were dressed in camouflage and bullet-proof vests, having decided from the beginning of this heist that they may not be able to return home. Dan looked at the lean guy next to the window. "What now, Jay?"

Jay was wired. "I'm takin' him out."

Without another word, he jumped out of the truck and ran toward the cruiser, aiming his SKS rifle straight at the cruiser's front windshield. He was shooting as he ran, amazed at the power of his bullets and getting a thrill out of glass being shattered and holes appearing in the cruiser's hood and doors. Nineteen shots were fired in rapid succession before he ran back to the truck.

Jumping in the passenger side, he whooped excitedly. "Go, Dan! That cop won't bother us now."

Dan shifted gears and stomped on the accelerator. "God, Jay! They'll be lookin' for us now. We gotta' get rid of this truck! We don't stand a chance in it."

Jay was ready for battle, and turned to the husky-looking guy beside him. "What do you think, Alec? Do we get another truck?"

Alec's face was now covered with a ski mask. "Whatever. Just go!"

Jay grinned, "Dan, head toward the landfill. I know a guy out there who has a fleet of trucks. We'll go in and take one of them, and no one better get in our way."

THREE

Cynthia waved good-bye to Matt and watched his black unmarked Jeep Cherokee disappear from view. Turning to go back inside, she suddenly felt like she was going to collapse! Clutching the door handle, she tried to steady herself. Her whole body was filled with a frightening sense of foreboding, and her heart began pounding wildly. It took all of her strength not to call Matt on his cell phone and tell him to come back.

For the first time since they had been together, she was overcome with a fear for his safety. The feeling grabbed at her throat, and she could barely breathe. *What if I never see him again?*

Swallowing hard, she tried to force herself to think more rationally. Cortez had a population of nine-thousand people and saw little crime other than a few burglaries or domestic cases, and of course, speeding tickets. But she also had to admit that since Matt had been appointed Head Detective at the sheriff's office, there had been several major busts over the last couple of years; murder cases that had made headlines.

Maybe she was just getting a delayed case of the jitters because of the big life change ahead of them. Once Matt attended the academy, he had no idea where he would be stationed. They might have to leave the lovely home they had built together and move to a big city like Denver.

However, none of that would bother Matt. He loved being a cop and was so good at his job. He would miss living in the mountains, but he would go wherever he was sent. And she would go with him.

She remembered the first time she had met Matt.

She had been hesitant about dating a cop because they didn't have the greatest of records for long-lasting relationships. She knew how they were always out there, trying to keep the populace safe so that individuals like her could sleep peacefully at night and drive the highways safely during the day.

She also knew they could be called out at any hour of the day or night and on holidays. Each time they put on their uniforms, they became a barrier between criminals and the public.

They had to wear body armor to protect themselves and often had to drive their cruisers at high speeds over dark mountain roads to either rescue or arrest someone. There were times they could be in danger from a suspect's blood or other body fluids.

She was also very aware of how friends and families of cops often receive threats from gangland murderers or militia-type groups. Apprehensive that a solid, healthy relationship could be possible with a cop, she was surprised at how attracted she was to him. He was maybe six-feet tall and had a solid, muscular build, but it was his twinkling blue eyes that got her attention.

After talking with him for just a brief time, she discovered he was not only a nice and decent person, but he was really easy to be around. They found themselves clicking like long-time friends.

He didn't exhibit any of the cockiness she had witnessed when around some of the other deputies in the office. Though Matt was certainly self-confident, he was also sweet and had a great sense of humor.

When he first asked her out to dinner, she accepted, and it was amazing how much they discovered they had in common. Both of them liked ZZ Top and jazz, they enjoyed nature and camping in the high mountains, and they shared a strong faith in God. She loved his strength, his honesty and the fact that he put family ahead of money. After life in the fast lane with her ex-husband, Matt had been like a breath of fresh air to her.

She thought back to one of their first dates when they had hiked up to Box Canyon Falls outside Ouray, a tiny mountain town north of Silverton. They had stood on a high ledge above the thundering water as it rushed into the deep recesses of the mountain, causing both of them to experience an almost mystical feeling of closeness.

The roar had been deafening as spray splattered their faces, dampening their hair and clothes. The limestone that the water surged over dated back to the beginning of the earth itself, and as she and Matt had stood there holding each other, she began feeling a sense of security she had not felt with any man before. They were unable to talk above the roar of the water, but they didn't need to. She knew at that moment they had a destiny together.

Clearing her mind as best she could, Cynthia forced herself to walk out to the kitchen for her grocery list. She needed to get ready for their long weekend celebration, and at the same time, she needed to shake the awful feelings that had almost knocked her to the floor.

FOUR

As Matt drove toward the sheriff's office, he rolled down the car window and breathed in the cool morning air. No rain had been predicted to spoil this perfect day or the coming weekend.

He was hoping he would be assigned to this same area once he completed the Colorado Highway Patrol Academy. He loved the land here. Remnants of the old west could be found everywhere in the Four Corners area. The rugged San Juans were Colorado's largest mountain range; a million acres of wilderness. A place you could get lost in if you wanted to.

He took his time getting to the office, contemplating what his last day at work would hold for him. He figured the guys would be throwing a little party for him today. Whenever someone quit or retired, that was the ritual. A cake, maybe a small gift, a few jokes and good luck wishes. He had his doubts about whether either the sheriff or Sanchez would make it, but that was just fine with him.. He knew he would miss the friends he had made over the last few years, but he also felt he had to move on.

As he drove by a small, neat house sitting back from the road, he recalled a disturbing murder case that had occurred there last year. A call had come in to dispatch from a distraut man who was sobbing that he had just returned from a trip and found his wife dead on the kitchen floor. Gasping for breath in-between his sobs, he had said blood was everywhere and that his wife had been shot in the head.

Deputies were immediately sent to the man's address, where they had entered the house with their guns drawn. They discovered the body of a young woman lying behind the breakfast bar in the kitchen. Since she had been shot two times in the face, they figured it had been personal and that the husband probably did it. The majority of murders are committed by family members or close friends.

Matt had arrived after the deputies, and as lead detective, secured the crime scene and conducted a preliminary investigation. Then he personally questioned the husband. The grieving man explained how he had left his wife and children to fly to Denver for a job interview the day before. He was scheduled to fly back to Durango that day, but due to flight problems, had been forced to fly to Cortez instead.

14

He told Matt his father was scheduled to pick him up in Durango, but he couldn't reach him on the phone to tell him to come to Cortez. Once he landed, he caught a ride to his house and found his wife dead. Looking at Matt, his face contorted in grief, he said, "Thank God my children are still in school!"

Matt nodded, but didn't say anything.

The man continued, "My Dad … he hated her. He always felt she was interfering with the family, and we've had some real problems with him. I haven't been able to reach him for hours." He closed his eyes. "He has a gun."

Matt had noticed a telephone bill sitting on the bar and saw that it had the father's name on it. Looking down at the slain woman, he felt anger welling up in him. What a senseless waste of life, and he made a silent promise to her right then. *I'm going to find out who did this to you and he's going to spend the rest of his life in prison.*

Matt obtained a "no-knock" search warrant for the father's house which allowed his team to bust the door down. It was an apartment complex for the elderly, and he was worried about tipping the old man off. Since the guy supposedly had a gun, he didn't want to take a chance on innocent people getting hurt.

The SWAT team had knocked the door down with a battering ram and caught the father in bed in his long johns and Tee shirt. Cuffing the ninety-year-old man, a deputy read him his rights and then sat him down on a chair. During this whole time, the old man didn't say one word. He just sat there silently starring at them as they bagged his clothes and shoes and other items for evidence.

When they bagged the old man's shoes, Matt had noticed what appeared to be high velocity blood spatters on them. Once they had finished their search, they took their suspect down to headquarters for interrogation.

Matt had begun by asking him, "What did you do this morning?"

He had scrunched up his face and said, "I went to City Market, and then I ate lunch. Then I went to the airport to pick up my son, but he wasn't there."

Matt said, "We knocked your door down, and you didn't ask us why. Any reason you didn't?"

As he stared at the man, Matt was thinking to himself, *"You did it, you SOB."*

When the man didn't answer, he asked, "Did you kill your daughter-in-law?"

The guy shook his head slowly. "No, no. There was never a time I'd do that."

Then he began talking about her in the past tense, admitting he had had problems accepting her and that he was seeing a counselor. Finally the tape recorder was turned off, and Matt asked, "If you killed her, would you tell me?"

He nodded. "Yeah, I'd tell you, but then I'd have to kill myself."

That was a play on the phrase 'I could tell you, but then I'd have to kill you.'

"Where's your gun?"

"I lost it. I took a woman out target shooting, and it got misplaced."

"How do you misplace a gun?"

The man shrugged his bony shoulders. "I'm not sure."

They had to let him go. Until their crime lab had a chance to go over all the evidence, they didn't have grounds to keep him in custody.

Two days later, the elderly man had shown up at the sheriff's office and said he wanted his wallet. He began complaining, saying his son was avoiding him. A deputy gave him his wallet, and he left.

On Saturday morning at six o'clock, the phone rang in Matt's house. He and Cynthia were still in bed, half-asleep, but he recognized the voice on the line as one of his deputies.

"You ain't gonna believe what just happened!"

Matt knew he meant the old man. "How'd he do it?"

"Went head on with a semi. The driver tried to avoid him, but couldn't."

The ninety-year-old man was cremated, but the family wouldn't claim his ashes. The urn sat in Matt's office for several months before being picked up by a relative.

The evidence that came back after his demise proved it was his daughter-in-law's blood on his shoes. Matt decided to visit the Southwest Mental Health Center in Durango and asked to see the guy's records since his privacy was no longer in jeopardy. The records turned out to be pretty revealing.

They told of his extreme hatred for his daughter-in-law, of how he was once a bootlegger and of a possible murder down in Texas. The man had been a loose cannon.

Now his son would live with the knowledge that his father's hatred had become so twisted and evil that he had killed his daughter-in-law in cold blood. The children no longer had a mother or a grandfather.

The husband of the murdered woman was a long-time friend of legendary country singer, Vince Gill, who had flown in for support and had stayed a month. The story had made national headlines, due in part to the presence of Vince Gill, and Sheriff Catlin loved every minute of it as he happily basked in the glory of all the publicity.

* * *

As Matt's Jeep sped toward the office for his last day there, all he felt was relief. He would be out of that atmosphere after today, and he was looking forward to a brand new start with the State Patrol. Of course, he had to get through the Academy first. Those who had already graduated liked to compare their experiences to being in boot camp, and though Matt had never been in the military, he had a pretty good idea of what lie ahead.

Sure, it would be difficult, but well worth doing to get out of the extremely political arena of the sheriff's office. He had already made plans to cash out his retirement benefits and take a month off before attending the academy.

As he pulled into the parking lot of the public building that housed the sheriff's office downtown, he noted it was exactly nine o'clock.

Walking through the double doors that led into the busy front hallway, Matt smiled as people greeted him and began ribbing him about it being his last day. He nodded and said, "Yeah, and you boys are gonna' miss me."

His comment led to a few choice remarks and some hoots of laughter.

Grinning, he headed back to his office when one of the secretaries intercepted him. "Matt, a staff meeting's been called and they want you there."

He thanked her and turned to head toward the conference room. As he entered the room, they were discussing what Detective Groggin's duties would be when he assumed the position of Detective Sergeant after Matt left.

Everyone greeted him as he made his way to the end of the long conference table. One deputy chuckled, saying, "About time you got here, Matt. Let's get this over with so we can have some of that cake I noticed in the break room."

Everyone laughed and Matt answered, "Hey, wait a minute. Don't I get the first piece of that cake?"

Another deputy answered, "Nope. You're leavin' us, so you have to wait at the end of the line."

Grinning, Matt sat down and had just started looking at some paperwork when the door slammed open, and an administrative assistant came rushing in, exclaiming, "There's an officer down! Out on the bridge at County Road 27!"

Chairs were pushed back and one toppled over as every man in the room scrambled to get up and rush to the door. Matt joined in the stampede, running out to his unmarked Jeep. Putting his strobe lights on, he activated the high beam headlights that flashed from right to left and sped off in the direction of the bridge.

As he and the others were enroute to the scene, a dispatcher's voice came over the radio, "The suspect's vehicle is a large water truck. Make that a large white water truck."

There was no information on how many suspects were involved or why the officer was down or even who the officer was. As his Jeep flew over the road, Matt found himself hoping it would be just a minor incident. Maybe the officer had pulled someone over, and the guy wasn't taking it well.

It was only nine-thirty in the morning, and it looked like he was going to spend his last day with the sheriff's office helping whoever was out there on that bridge.

The three survivalists spied a guy driving a flatbed truck just as he was pulling out of a lot near the landfill. Dan quickly positioned the water truck in front of the flatbed truck, preventing it from exiting onto the road. Jay jumped out and stuck his rifle in the driver's face. "Get out! Now!"

The guy couldn't get the door open fast enough as he leaped to the ground and took off running. Laughing, Jay and Dan scrambled up into the cab of the flatbed while Alec pointed to the bed of the truck. "I'll ride shotgun."

FIVE

Arriving at the bridge, Matt saw a white police car sitting on the side of the road, its windows completely shot out, glass strewn everywhere. Several fire department volunteers were already on the scene, which told him how serious the situation was.

Slowing down, he started to pull over when a dispatcher came back on the radio. "The water truck has been spotted going north on County Road 25."

He was easily within a mile of that road. Seeing that the downed officer was in competent hands, he made the decision to head south toward the last sighting of the truck. Since he was in an unmarked vehicle, it would give him a decent chance of apprehending the suspect before the guy saw he was a cop. Turning off his lights, he advised dispatch of his plan and pulled back on the road to turn south.

Something that made him nervous was the extensive damage done to the patrol car at the bridge. Some kind of high caliber semi-automatic weapon had totally shattered the cruiser's windows. He reached back behind his seat and grabbed his bullet-proof vest, threw it over his head and quickly fastened the straps. He wanted to be as prepared as he could be in case things got crazy really fast.

As he approached the intersection where he could turn onto CR 25, he saw a turquoise car speeding through the same intersection heading south. The car was swerving all over the road, and Matt recognized the car as belonging to the Assistant Chief of Police. *What the heck was he doing?*

He would find out later that the Chief had been desperately searching for his gun, which was somewhere on the floorboard under the seat.

Matt headed south on CR 25, knowing the road eventually led to residential homes and then intersected with Highway 666. He spied two police cars directly ahead of him and realized they were heading in the same direction, where the road would eventually end at the County landfill.

Since they were already going south, he decided to turn west so they wouldn't all be going in the same direction. He had gone about a mile when he encountered a man standing in the middle of the road, waving his arms in the air.

Recognizing him as someone who lived in the immediate area, he stopped the Jeep and rolled down the window. The man ran up to Matt's Jeep and exclaimed breathlessly, "That truck you're looking for didn't come this way! I've been listening to my police scanner, and I've been lookin' for it. It has *not* come this way."

Matt nodded. "Thanks! I appreciate it."

He had quickly turned his Jeep around in the road and headed back to CR 25, where he turned south once more. As he exited onto CR 25, he heard radio traffic coming from patrol cars up ahead. Somebody was shouting over sounds that he assumed were gunfire. "Shots are being fired! We have officers in trouble!"

He heard screaming in the background and the sound of more shots, then someone yelled out that the suspect was heading north on CR 25. That was just minutes ahead of him! The guys on the radio were probably the two working units he had seen a bit earlier when he had turned into the residential area.

He stomped on the accelerator, feeling the car practically jump down the highway. A few moments later, he saw two kids on bicycles appear out of nowhere and fear shot through him. With those kids in the vicinity of the approaching truck, he knew it would be difficult to protect them and apprehend the suspect at the same time. This would definitely limit his options!

Someone was yelling on the radio again. He heard loud static and then someone shouted something like "…. northbound on 25!"

Now he knew for certain the suspect was heading straight toward him, and those kids were right in their path. They had no idea what was coming their way and it was up to him to stop that truck before it got that far!

Adrenaline kicked in and he yanked his shotgun down from where it was mounted to the roof of the Jeep and laid it on his lap. He wanted that gun where he could get to it fast. It was a short-barreled shotgun with a folding stock; only two feet long, but an efficient, deadly weapon.

Coming around a curve in the road, he spied a yellow-and-white flatbed truck come flying over the hill straight at him, and he instantly recognized the truck as one owned by a local company next to the landfill. Evidently the suspect had abandoned the water truck and stolen this one. Why hadn't dispatch broadcast that information? With the flatbed truck moving at such an alarming rate of speed, he was amazed the driver could keep it on the road.

Calling in this information to dispatch, his Jeep and the truck were now almost upon one another. Matt was rapidly using up the options he had left. If he collided with the truck, he could stop it right then. *But that would kill me and whoever is in the truck!*

He could use the passenger's side of his Jeep to sideswipe the truck, which should cause it to crash. *Won't work. We're both goin' too fast.*

A small church came into view and he made the split-second decision to turn into its driveway. He could position his Jeep halfway out into the road and, in theory, force the suspect to stop. Then he could bail out with his shotgun and the chase would be over.

Keenly aware he was probably in for an across-the-hood shootout, he felt confident that his shotgun would stop the suspect. Yanking the steering wheel to the left, he caused the Jeep to slide halfway into the driveway. Once he got the Jeep positioned to where it was blocking the narrow road, he slammed on the brakes and pushed it into park.

As he rolled out of the car, keeping his head low, he managed to keep his shotgun on his lap. Grabbing the gun, he spun around and slammed the Jeep's door shut behind him. Once he was in position to see over the hood, he took a quick look and at that instant, bullets began flying and he stepped into hell.

SIX

How long had it been since he'd made the decision to turn into the church driveway? Five minutes? Ten? An hour? Now he was lying under his Jeep, badly wounded, with little protection from the deadly bullets that were zipping within inches of his body.

Sometimes your fate depends on a resident angel that God sends your way, and hopefully being trapped in the driveway of a small country church might catch His attention. He needed all the help he could get because, at any moment, one of those bullets might hit him in the head and that would be it.

As those thoughts flew through the haze of his pain, he said a prayer for his wife and family and prepared to die. Instead, a miracle happened. The bullets stopped and everything turned deathly still.

He continued lying under the Jeep without moving, all senses on high alert, listening to its motor amazingly still running after being blasted by bullets over and over. He gradually became aware of green radiator fluid pouring down in front of him, which caused a surreal sound similar to a running river.

Cautiously raising his head while trying not to touch the hot undercarriage of the Jeep, Matt could see the mountains rising up beyond the canyonlands, looking distorted through the heat of the sweltering sun. Dust still floated in the air from the recent barrage of bullets. Just beyond the Jeep a small whirling dust devil was kicking up its heels and sweat was pouring down his face and neck as he strained to hear movement of any kind.

The total silence indicated no one was waiting to kill him. Gingerly maneuvering his battered body around, he decided to risk looking out from behind the front tire. Nothing. They were gone.

He dropped back on the hard ground and took a deep breath. Maybe he was going to make it after all. First he had to get out from under the Jeep and radio for help. Gritting his teeth, knowing it was going to hurt like hell, he managed to scoot on his stomach and pull himself forward with his right arm. His left arm was useless, and his right knee wouldn't bend. Every movement he made caused excruciating pain to his arm and leg, but at last he emerged into the open.

When he automatically tried to thrust his left arm out for leverage, it barely moved. It was at that moment he saw how badly he was bleeding. Each time he moved, blood spurted out like a small fountain. He froze where he was, and as he waited for help to arrive, he could hear his heart pumping and watched as a steady stream of fresh blood, *his* blood, flowed into the dirt.

The sun was burning against Matt's wounded arm, and flies were beginning to gather around his wounds when a shadow flickered across his face. Startled, he looked up to see a large, muscular figure looming over him.

The large apparition spoke to him, "It's okay, buddy. You're gonna' be all right. But you're bleeding pretty bad. We need to get it stopped right away!"

Matt squinted and recognized Waylon Jones, a young Navajo Officer with the local city police department. He knew things were going to be alright now. The six-foot, barrel-chested officer reached down and placed his big hand under Matt's upper arm, then squeezed hard. He was putting a pressure point grip on Matt's artery just above the bullet wound, and the arterial blood flow instantly stopped.

Waylon tried to sound calm, but his voice was shaky. "I gotta' get you some help, Matt."

Matt slowly nodded his head. "Thanks, Waylon. I tried to get to the radio …."

Waylon cut him off and began looking around frantically. "Where's your first-aid kit?"

Matt's strength was ebbing. "Call an …."

Waylon cut him off again, "Where's that first-aid kit?"

Realizing Waylon was almost in shock himself, Matt raised his voice, "I need an **ambulance**, Waylon!"

The big officer looked frightened. "I know that! Okay, you're gonna' have to reach over and pinch off your artery like I'm doing. Can you do that, buddy?"

Grimacing, Matt nodded. "I think so."

Grasping his left arm in the same place Waylon had, Matt squeezed as hard as he could. He managed to keep a tight enough grip on his arm to keep the blood from spilling into the dirt again while Waylon used the Jeep's radio to order an ambulance. Matt was surprised it still worked.

From his peripheral vision, he saw other officers pulling up in their cars. Doors slammed and he heard the sound of running feet coming toward him. Then he was looking up into the shocked faces of several local cops. They gasped when they first spied him lying in a huge pool of blood pinching off his own artery, but quickly gained their composure.

They tried to appear calm by encouraging him with small talk while waiting for Waylon to get off the radio. Then more officers arrived. He would have laughed if he'd had the strength when he startled them by saying, "Hey, did you get those guys yet?"

They must have assumed he was dead when they initially saw all the blood. It surprised him when no one offered him assistance with his arm. They all stood there in a circle, looking down at him while he was struggling to keep a tight pressure grip above his left elbow. When Waylon finally got off the Jeep's radio to say an ambulance was on the way, one state trooper said his car was disabled from gunshots and asked Waylon is he could borrow his cruiser.

Waylon looked at Matt and nodded. "Yeah. I'm staying here with him."

The Trooper wished Matt good luck, then took off running toward Waylon's car. The remaining officers were now anxious to leave also, so giving him a few encouraging words, they quickly took off to join in the pursuit of the killers.

Waylon once more took over holding his arm, while Matt closed his eyes and thought about his family. *"I'm going to make it through this. And then I've got a camping trip to go on."*

SEVEN

Twenty minutes earlier, before they encountered Matt, the fleeing survivalists were speeding down County Road F when they spied a sheriff's deputy in a cruiser directly ahead of them. They pulled up as close to the cruiser's bumper as they could, and Jay leaned out the window and opened fire. The deputy slumped over the steering wheel and the cruiser went off the road, crashing into a fence.

Jay yelled above the noise of the wind as they sped by the cruiser. "Got another one!"

Skidding around a sharp bend where CR F connected with CR 25, the trio saw a Colorado State Patrol cruiser coming toward them. Alec, lying flat on the bed of the truck, opened fire as the trooper's car passed by. The bullets flattened the cruiser's tires and shattered its windshield, disabling it.

Before they could congratulate themselves, another sheriff's cruiser rounded the corner and they quickly emptied bullets into it, also disabling it. Yet another cruiser came at them, and once more they opened fire, but missed this time. Within minutes, they came over a hill to find their way blocked by a Jeep and a deputy holding a big shotgun.

Dan stepped on the accelerator and managed to squeeze around the Jeep, exposing the deputy as he crouched down beside the fender of his vehicle. Jay and Alec fired off forty rounds at the deputy, hitting him in the arm and leg just as he made a dive for the undercarriage of the Jeep.

Jay shouted, "We got him! Stop so we can finish him off!"

*Dan exclaimed, "If we don't keep movin' we're dead ourselves! That cop we just passed back there will be tellin' everyone where we are and what we're driving. We gotta' get to the canyonlands **now**!"*

They reached the intersection of CR 25 and CR G where they encountered another sheriff's car. They hit it with a large volley of bullets and watched the deputies yank their cruiser off the road and hit the floor. That would later turn out to be Captain Juan Sanchez and two sheriff's deputies.

Jay looked in the side mirror and yelled, "Damn! We got four more cruisers behind us!"

Dan yelled back, "I got it floored!"

As they neared the intersection of CR G and US 160, Jay and Alec fired bullets at a car and a garbage truck. Panicked drivers trying to get out of the way of the flatbed truck ended up stopping all traffic and the cruisers pursuing them were trapped in the ensuing entanglement of cars.

Looking in the rearview mirror, Dan laughed excitedly. "Good shootin', Jay! I think we're gonna' make it."

Jay chuckled, "Damn, you should see 'em back there! It'll take those cops an hour to unsnarl that mess."

They continued on CR G up into McElmo Canyon, then doubled back on Pleasant View Road and headed east toward Hovenweep National Monument on the border of Utah and Colorado. Feeling safer, Dan asked. "How many cops do you think we got?"

Jay shrugged his shoulders. "Not nearly enough."

Suddenly Dan was nervous again. "We lost them for now, but you know they're on their radios tellin' the world where we're headed. You sure we're gonna' make it?"

"Hell, yes, we are! This is what we've been trainin' for." He turned to face his buddy. "You're not gettin' cold feet, are you, Dan?

"No! We're gettin' ready for the end of the world, and I want to be a part of all that. But that cop we just shot ... the one who rolled under his car. He's dead, ain't he?"

"How should I know? You're the one who didn't want to stop and make sure. One cop, twenty cops. What difference does it make? It's cops like him that's caused the world to be in the mess it's in."

Dan slowly nodded. "I know."

The radio started crackling, and Jay held up his hand. "Shut up! Listen! They got roadblocks set up out on 666. Good! They don't know where we are!"

As Dan slowed the truck down to make a sharp turn, Jay leaned out the window and shouted back to the husky man lying on the flatbed of the truck. "You doin' okay back there, Alec?"

"Yeah! How much farther?"

"Not much. They got roadblocks on 666, so they don't know where we are!"

Alec just nodded, hunkering down against the hot wind.

They were almost to the entrance of the Hovenweep National Park entrance when Dan yelled out, "Cop ahead!"

The park ranger spotted them at the same time, and immediately drove his government car into a ditch and hit the floor. As the flatbed truck sped by the stalled car, Jay fired at it from the passenger window and Alec joined in from the bed of the truck.

Knowing the ranger had probably used his radio to broadcast their location, Dan hit the accelerator and headed toward their predetermined destination.

* * *

Matt was surprised at how fast the ambulance was on the scene and very appreciative of their bravery by coming into a "hot" zone to get him. It turned out that the ambulance driver was a hazardous material state trooper who was working in the area.

A tourniquet was immediately applied to Matt's mangled arm and, as the ambulance crew scooped him onto a backboard to load him into the rear of the ambulance, Matt grasped Waylon's hand. "Thanks. You saved my life."

Waylon nodded as Matt was pushed into the back of the ambulance, and the young Navajo officer stood still while the driver shut the doors. With sirens blaring, the ambulance was quickly on its way to the hospital in Cortez.

The ride to town was rough, and Matt found himself clinging tightly to the back board with his uninjured hand as the ambulance bounced and swayed over the bumpy County road.

In the midst of this bedlam, the young paramedic working on his arm said, "Sorry, Detective Nelson, but I need to start an IV. That means I'm gonna' have to stick you, Sir."

Matt raised his eyebrow and tried to smile. "I think I can handle that."

The guy nodded in sympathy, his eyes telling Matt how serious his wounds were. He had difficulty getting the IV started and once it was in, Matt was struck with an even greater pain in his injured arm.

Gritting his teeth, he asked, "Any chance you can give me something for the pain?"

He patted Matt's shoulder. "I'm giving you some morphine in your IV. It should help until we get to the hospital."

The morphine momentarily took the edge off, but by the time the ambulance pulled up in front of the emergency room, Matt's left arm was throbbing with the most excruciating pain he had ever felt in his life. His knee was more numb than painful and didn't compare to his arm, which now felt like someone was in the process of sawing it off.

He had remained clear-headed during the ride in the ambulance and had not yet experienced any time distortion or tunnel vision. He wasn't talking in slow motion as is often the case in badly wounded people, so he clung to that as a good sign. Yet he also knew he was in bad shape and that things could turn in a matter of minutes.

The trauma medical team was waiting by the emergency door for them and instantly rushed out to help the paramedics get him inside. Sliding him out of the back of the ambulance onto a stretcher, they rapidly wheeled him through the front lobby of the ER where their faces reflected the horror of knowing what he had just been through.

He was aware that the hospital had police scanners and guessed that the staff had been following the whole scene as it was playing out. As they were pushing him through the double doors that led to the ER rooms, the nurses began bombarding him with questions. He managed to raise his head from the stretcher and said, "First I need someone to call my wife."

While he waited to be seen by a specialist, the staff was keeping a close watch on his arm but seemed to be ignoring his leg injury. Finally he asked, "What about my leg? It's beginning to hurt pretty damned bad."

The nurse who had cut away his shirt looked at him in confusion. "Your leg?"

The paramedics had covered his leg with a blanket and though the blood from his wound had started seeping through, no one seemed too interested in it yet. When the nurse threw the blanket aside, her eyes widened as she saw all the blood now leaking onto the bed. She quickly began cutting the pant leg open and pushed a button for help, exclaiming, "This should have been taken care of immediately!"

Another nurse came rushing in with a tray of bandages and cleaning supplies. A portable X-ray machine was rolled in, along with an oxygen tank He was soon so bound up in bandages, IV's and the oxygen mask and tubes, he couldn't move.

As he lay there waiting for word on the severity of his wounds, the nurse told him the officer whose car had been heavily blasted out there on the bridge had been killed outright. She said he hadn't stood a chance. Another sheriff's deputy had also been shot, but he had a head wound, and the extent of his injuries weren't known yet..

Finally a doctor entered Matt's room and explained to him that they were putting him on standby until the deputy with the head wound had stabilized and been evaluated. Matt was acutely aware of what those rifles were capable of and being shot in the head had been his greatest fear. He said a silent prayer for both officers' families, knowing what they must be going through.

It seemed time was crawling at a snail's pace as he lay there waiting to hear what was being decided. Finally the doctor came back in the room and informed him they were now considering flying him to Denver, but had not made a decision yet. He said he had ordered Air Care to be on standby.

The doctor also informed him he had lost fifty percent of his body's blood since he'd been shot. He was incredulous. "Fifty! Uh, maybe I'm wrong on this, but can't you die if you lose just forty percent of your blood?"

The tall, craggy-faced doctor nodded his head. "That's usually the case, but you are a very lucky man, Detective Nelson. The young officer who stopped the arterial blood flow when he did literally saved your life."

A nurse had entered the room in time to hear what the doctor had said. She reached out and patted his right hand. "You must have a guardian angel watching over you, Detective."

He couldn't smile because of the oxygen mask, but he tried. "Yeah. I know I've got a lot to be grateful for."

Even though it was only ten in the morning on what was to have been his last day on the job, he had become one of the first casualties of a vicious war that was still far from being over. He figured he wouldn't be the last either.

EIGHT

Cynthia had not been able to shake the alarming feeling of emptiness that had hit her when Matt left. Anxious to get out of the house, she drove to their church near Dolores to print the Sunday bulletin, but found it physically impossible to open the car door. A feeling of urgency was building in her, causing her lungs to tighten like they were being squeezed in a vise. Slamming the car back in gear, she sped out of the driveway and headed in the direction of her mother's house. *She had to talk to Matt.*

Once she reached her mother's house, she rushed up to the front door and pushed it open. With a quick greeting to her surprised mother, she ran to the phone in the kitchen and quickly dialed the number of the cell phone in Matt's Jeep. When no one answered, she pushed in the number to the sheriff's office.

She was immediately transferred to a dispatcher who told her Matt and most of the officers from the station were out due to an emergency. Cynthia hung up the phone and stared at her confused-looking mother, unable to voice what her heart was telling her. Without a word, she dialed dispatch again.

This time the dispatcher's voice was tense. "Sorry, Mrs. Nelson, but there's been a shooting. We have officers down. We'll have to call you back."

Cynthia slowly hung up, her throat constricting in fear as she looked at her mother. Instantly her feelings of anxiety became crystal clear, and she could barely breathe.

Her mother's hands began fluttering in nervousness as she asked, "Cynthia, what's wrong?"

The sound of the ringing phone cut between them and Cynthia quickly grabbed for the receiver. "Hello?"

A female caller asked, "Is this Mrs. Matt Nelson?"

It was the hospital.

Cynthia ran out to her car with her mother close behind. Jumping in, she turned the key in the car's ignition and switched the emergency flashers on as her mother climbed onto the passenger seat. Both of them snapped their seat belts on, and Cynthia pressed the accelerator to the floor while praying everyone would stay out of her way. From the corner of her eye, she saw her mother clinging to the door handle for dear life.

At one point, they went racing past a car and her mother screamed out in fright, "Cynthia! Slow down! Matt is alive and he needs you alive too!"

Cynthia couldn't answer her mother. Her whole being was focused on getting to the hospital. When they reached the emergency entrance, she yanked the wheel toward the curved driveway, causing the tires to squeal loudly. Slamming on her brakes, lights still flashing, she found her hands were shaking so badly she could barely get the car turned off.

Grabbing her purse, she motioned to her mother. "Come on, Mom! Let's go!"

She jumped out of the car, leaving the lights still flashing, and led her mother into the ER lobby. Fearfully approaching the front desk, breathless from her tightened lungs, she identified herself and asked to see her husband.

As the nurse looked at Cynthia, she suddenly nodded in recognition. "Yes, Mrs. Nelson! We've been expecting you. Let me get someone to take you to your husband, but first, would you like me to request a chaplain to come and talk with you?"

Cynthia's eyes widened with trepidation and she could barely get her words out, "Why would I need a chaplain? Matt's not ... dead, is he?"

The nurse immediately realized her error. "No! No, he's badly wounded, but the doctors are working to ..."

At that moment, Cynthia caught sight of a blanket-clad man lying in a small room down the hall with one muscular, pale-looking leg sticking out from under the covers.

She pointed to the room. "That's him! That's my husband!"

Ignoring the nurse, she walked purposely down the hall and entered the tiny, private room. She saw Matt swathed in bandages with tubes everywhere and an oxygen mask covering his mouth and nose. The only thing that kept her on her feet were his blue eyes looking straight at her, showing his happiness at seeing her.

He tried to raise up a bit, but the oxygen mask was inhibiting both his movements and his speech. "Hi, baby."

Tears came to her eyes, and she rushed to the side of the narrow bed to gently take his unbandaged hand. "I got here as fast as I could, Honey."

She felt like she had walked into a world alien to everything she knew and found herself crowding as close to Matt as she could physically get. His face looked chalky and had a yellow pallor about it, but he was alive. That's what she would concentrate on right at that moment.

* * *

As soon as Cynthia had walked through the door, Matt felt his body relax a bit. Even though her face was drawn and her eyes wide with fright, she looked like an angel coming toward him.

She leaned down and kissed his forehead, the only spot available on his face. With tears in her eyes, she said, "I should have called you back this morning. I should never have let you go to work."

His eyes looked confused. "I don't understand."

"I had this awful feeling the minute you walked out the door. I tried to go to church, but I couldn't get out of the car and I went to Mom's to call you. Except I couldn't get you on your cell phone and then dispatch said an officer was down and …"

"Cynthia … I would have gone anyway."

She was silent for a moment, then slowly nodded her head. "I know." She touched his bandaged arm, but her eyes immediately focused on his leg. "They said it was just your arm! What's wrong with your leg?"

"When they called you, I don't think they knew how bad my leg was."

She looked alarmed. "Why not?"

"The paramedic had covered it with a blanket, and I know the nurses were concentrating on my arm. Until I said something, I guess they weren't aware of how bad it was."

Cynthia frowned and clasped his uninjured arm. "How could they miss it?"

A nurse suddenly entered the room and said, "Detective Nelson, the doctor has decided you won't be flown out after all. He's going to operate on you right now, so I need to prep you."

She glanced at Cynthia. "I'm sorry, Mrs. Nelson, but I'm going to need you to stand over there."

Cynthia nodded, but she was hesitant about leaving Matt for even a minute. She needed to see and understand everything they were going to do to her husband, especially after hearing about his leg.

She watched and listened as the nurse administered a shot to Matt's right arm, explaining how it would relax him before he went into surgery. As the nurse was prepping him, a tall doctor with compassionate eyes entered the room and smiled at Matt. "We're going to operate on that arm and leg now, Matt."

Matt introduced him to Cynthia, then grinned crookedly and said, "Just make sure the arm's still there when I wake up, okay?."

The doctor did not smile back. "I'm going to do my best, Matt."

Matt's eyes met Cynthia's shocked ones. "I know you will." He paused, then tried to make a joke. "Well, if I have to go through life being called Stumpy, so be it."

He saw that Cynthia didn't think it was funny. He beckoned her over and took her hand. "Honey, it's going to be okay."

She looked at him with swollen eyes. "I know. God was with you when you faced those killers, and He'll be with you in the operating room."

The medicine was now causing his voice to slightly slur. "You got that right, Honey."

As they prepared to wheel Matt out of the room, Cynthia felt panic rush through her and she turned to the nurse, "Please! I need to be with him. I promise not to get in anyone's way."

The nurse was sympathetic but firm. "I understand, Mrs. Nelson, but we cannot allow you to do that."

Cynthia felt tears of frustration well up in her eyes. "You won't even know I'm there. Please let me go with him!"

The nurse slowly shook her head. "I'm sorry."

An aide began pushing Matt's bed toward the door, and Cynthia ran over to him to grasp his hand. By this time, the medication they had given Matt was causing him to fade fast. He mumbled, "Don't worry, Baby."

She had to let go of his hand as they pushed his bed through the narrow door, but she kept pace with them until they reached the doors that led to surgery. The nurse was suddenly in front of her. "This is as far as you can go. I'm sorry."

Matt was barely conscious, but he knew how determined his wife could be. He was so drowsy he had a hard time forming his words, but he somehow managed to wink and said, "See you … soon."

As the doors shut blocking out her view of Matt, Cynthia was beside herself. The nurse who had stopped her from entering the surgery room now smiled gently. "He's in good hands, Mrs. Nelson."

Cynthia stood there, feeling helpless and lost. Her whole world had changed within the space of an hour, and she was now entrusting the life of her husband to doctors she knew nothing about. It was very frightening. What if Matt came out minus a leg or arm? He had always been such a physical man and being a cop required him to be in top physical condition.

If he was forced to take a desk job back in that environment he had been so anxious to leave, how would he cope? She had heard of badly wounded police officers who were left crippled for life becoming hard and bitter.

Matt was such a kind, sweet man with a wonderful zest for life. Would the doctors save his life only to have him lose sight of who he was? She shook her head. No, even if he lost his arm, he could still do everything he had been doing. And she would be right there by his side. *But what if he loses his leg?*

She squeezed her eyes tightly shut and tried to stop her spinning, out-of-control thoughts. *Faith. She had to have faith.*

Matt was in God's capable hands, and whatever decisions were being reached behind those closed doors, they would be the right ones. Taking a deep breath, she turned and began slowly walking toward the small waiting room adjacent to the surgery area where her mother had gone.

NINE

When they first wheeled Matt into the operating room, the doctors were skeptical of the outcome of the surgery. They knew they had to operate right then if there was to be any chance at all of saving his arm. There was a good possibility he would lose it since the bullet had ripped away extensive muscle and flesh from his forearm and biceps and the doctors were keenly aware of the lengthy operation they had ahead of them.

* * *

Five hours later, one of Matt's doctors came into the waiting room where Cynthia and her mother waited. Cynthia clasped her mother's hand and anxiously searched his face for what he was about to tell them. When he slowly smiled, she knew the operation had been a success. Still holding her mother's hand in hers, she listened to the details of Matt's wounds and how they had literally pieced him back together again.

By the time he finished telling them what he knew, tears had begun forming in Cynthia's eyes again, this time in joy. She stood up and impulsively hugged the doctor, thanking him at least twice before turning to her mother and tightly embracing her.

Her mother was crying too, and said, "I knew the good Lord wouldn't take our Matt from us."

* * *

He could barely open his eyes, and his mouth felt as dry as cotton. When he tried to clear his throat, a dry, hacking cough erupted. A nurse immediately appeared at his side. "It's okay, Detective Nelson. The dryness is from the medicine. Do you feel nauseous?"

He shook his head, unable to talk yet. She patted his hand. "Let me get you some ice."

All he could think about at that moment was that he had survived the surgery. He slowly turned his head and apprehensively looked at his left arm.

Relief rushed through him when he saw *fingers* beyond the thick bandage! He still had his arm!

Next he checked his leg. At first it was difficult to see due to all the bandages and tubes linked to his IV and oxygen tank. He thought it looked about the right length, so he positioned his head for a better view and saw his foot! The leg and foot were both still there!

Grateful beyond belief, he closed his eyes and said a silent prayer. *Thank you, Lord. I was really worried there for awhile.*

When his doctor eventually walked into the recovery room, a big grin dominated his face. "Hi, Matt. Well, you really put us through our paces. We had to do a lot of repair work, and you're going to be in rehab for quite awhile, but we managed to save both the leg and the arm. The fact that you were in such excellent physical condition helped a lot."

Matt gave him a weak "thumbs up" and said, "I can't thank you enough. I admit I had my doubts, but you did it. I'm in your debt."

"Hey, that's what we're here for. Now, you need to know there's been a lot of damage done to your arm, and it's going to require several skin grafts over the next week. The bullet in your knee split the head of the tibia bone into five pieces, so we're not sure just how much that will affect your walking abilities in the future."

Matt nodded, "I understand. I'm just glad my arm and leg are still with me. I'm sort of used to having them around."

The doctor looked exhausted, but he grinned and patted Matt on the shoulder. "Understood. Now, as soon as you're stabilized, we'll transfer you to your room. I have it on good authority that Mrs. Nelson is waiting for you."

Matt grinned back. "I have no doubt of that."

When the doctor left, Matt rested his head on the small hospital pillow, floating between pain and the oblivion of morphine. He *would* walk again and then he was going to the academy, one way or the other.

* * *

Once Matt's vital signs stabilized, they transferred him to a private room in the Intensive Care Unit. Cynthia was waiting for him, her eyes shining through tears as she looked up from the chair where she had been impatiently waiting for him. Rushing over to his bed as they wheeled it into position, she quickly kissed him and said, "They saved your arm and leg, Baby. You're going to make it now. You're going to be fine."

Though his eyes felt heavy, he reached out for her hand. "I've got a lot to be thankful for."

He slept off and on for the next few hours, and when he awoke later that evening, he was so thirsty he could barely swallow. Cynthia went out into the hall to flag down a passing attendant and asked for some water. Within minutes, a young nurse walked in carrying a tray with a jug of ice water and a glass. Sitting them on the table next to his bed, she pushed a button which caused the head of the bed to rise. Helping him to sit up straighter, she asked, "How are you feeling, Detective Nelson?"

He was still groggy and his mouth seemed to have a hard time moving. "Not too bad. Still pretty doped up though."

He was surprised when tears suddenly appeared in the nurse's dark eyes. Her voice trembled as she said, "I'm so sorry about what happened to you, Detective Nelson. I was just told that one of those guys the police are looking for …. it is my cousin, Alec Column."

He saw how her hands were trembling, and she quickly turned her head away from him as though she was ashamed to meet his eyes. At that moment, Cynthia walked over and placed her arm around the young woman's shoulders. "Hey, we appreciate you telling us this, but *you* are not to blame for what your cousin did."

Matt felt sorry for her. "You don't need to take on his guilt. He made his own decision to get involved in this mess."

The woman had a stricken look on her face. "I'm sorry. I shouldn't have come in here and told you that. I hope I didn't upset you. I … I just wanted to tell you how sorry I am." She started to leave then turned back. "I pray you get well soon, Detective Nelson."

She silently slipped through the door and was gone.

Matt and Cynthia looked at each other and Matt predicted, "If those guys *are* local boys, there's going to be a lot of families around here wondering why."

TEN

During the first two days of Matt's recovery, he remained drugged and groggy most of the time, alternating between pain and extreme weakness. He was always pleased when any of the city police officers dropped in on him because it helped get his mind on something other than the pain.

Waylon Jones, the officer who had literally saved his life by stopping the blood flow from his arm, walked in his room on the day after his operation. The big Navajo grinned down at him and extended his hand. "Hey, buddy! I was glad to hear the operation was a success."

Matt shook his hand and smiled. "Thanks, Waylon. Sit down and tell me what's going on out there."

The officer sat in the chair next to Matt, his large frame filling up the tiny space between the bed and the window. "We haven't caught 'em yet, Matt. I don't know how they got through all our roadblocks and helicopter surveillances. When I first heard we had an officer down, I headed toward the landfill thinkin' that could be one of the places they might head. Right about then, I saw that flatbed truck goin' north and literally flyin'. There were two guys in the cab and one was lyin' flat on the bed. I knew they had to be the ones we were lookin' for. They fired off some rounds at Deputy Pope by gettin' behind him, and then they tried to get me as they drove by, but missed."

Waylon shifted in the chair, looking uncomfortable. "I guess you know about Pope bein' shot in the head. He was finally flown to Barrow's in Phoenix, and it's a miracle he's okay. Anyway, as I said, those guys went barreling past me and fired some shots off, but didn't hit me. I turned my cruiser around, and when I came over that hill, I saw your Jeep halfway out in the road and you outside the car. I saw you get mowed down by bullets while you were tryin' to get under the Jeep. Damn, I thought for sure you were dead!"

Matt took a deep breath. "Yeah, me too."

Waylon shook his head. "When I saw all that blood comin' outta' your arm and that big hole in your elbow … man, the only thing I could think about was tryin' to stop the blood. quick."

"And you did, buddy. You helped save my life."

The young officer looked down at the floor. "I came close to losin' it when I saw how bad it was."

Matt nodded somberly. "All I know is that you're my hero, friend."

And he meant it.

* * *

While Matt was still in ICU following the shootings, a couple of deputies from his department and several officers from other police departments dropped by his room to give him some encouraging words. Then they would leave.

Sheriff Catlin, Sergeant Juan Sanchez and Undersheriff Warner neither came to see him, nor did they call. Detective Groggin, the one who was taking over Matt's position in the department, was also a no-show. He was ignored so completely by his department that no one was even sent to take a report from him on the shooting.

He received flowers and cards from other police departments, but nothing from his own supervisors, and it bothered him a lot. Was it just a lack of compassion on their parts, or did they consider him already gone? Even though he had quit, it should not have made a difference. Yeah, it had been his last day with the department, but he was a cop and went out to do his job. He had almost lost his life that day and was now facing one of the biggest battles of his life. The least the sheriff could do was pick up the phone and wish him well.

Cynthia stayed at the hospital with him every day, refusing to leave his side for any length of time. She kept asking him why no one from the sheriff's office had called or visited the hospital. She really expected the wives to show up and give her some encouraging words, but with each passing day, he saw her getting more confused and upset. He found himself more upset for her than for himself. Damn it, his wife needed their support too. What the hell was going on?

After the doctors performed the painful skin grafts on his arm, Cynthia confessed to him that she was angry at their lack of support. "I am so mad! Don't they care that you're lying here struggling to survive? That you're in such pain you can't move! The whole department should be standing around this bed right now, telling you what a great cop you are! It was your last day and you didn't have to be out there. But because you are such a good cop, you went out to stop those creeps. And now your own department isn't here to support you. Why not?"

He tried to act like it was no big deal for her sake. "Maybe it's because it was my last day with the department. Maybe … I don't really know, Cynthia."

She decided to make some discreet inquiries concerning what his department had done for the other officers who had been wounded in the shootings. What she discovered caused her to be more upset than before. Sheriff Catlin and his administration had not only sent flowers to the slain officer's family, but also cards had been sent to Deputy Pope and the other officers who had been wounded. Only Matt and his family had been totally left out.

When she told Matt what she had found out, he shook his head. It was beyond his comprehension. "Just goes to show you that I made a good decision to get the hell out of that group when I did. Let it go, Cynthia. It's not worth it."

But it still hurt.

Later that week, two deputies from his department dropped by his room, but Matt felt they had come to ask questions about his future plans after rehab more than anything else. How did they expect him to answer intelligently about his future at this point in time? All he wanted to do right then was survive. Nothing they said gave him a sense of any real concern for his well-being.

Officers from other police departments, like Waylon Jones and those with the highway patrol, were sincere in offering encouragement as he lay there day after day. So why were the deputies he had taken the same oath with and who had pinned on the same badge as he now keeping their distances? He thought of all the times he had gone to bat for those under him, and it left him feeling empty.

Thank God for Greg Watson, the Highway Patrol Sergeant stationed in Durango, who continued to keep him updated with phone calls. Each time they talked, he encouraged him to hurry up and get well because they were holding his position open at the academy. It was his kindness that was keeping Matt's dreams alive.

Eventually a phone call did come through from personnel at the sheriff's office. A lady from bookkeeping nonchalantly informed him he was still on the county payroll because he had been hurt while on the job. Without one inquiry about his injuries, she told him he would be receiving papers to sign. Then she hung up.

Not even the bookkeeper gave a damn about his injuries. Matt had always been conscious of the dangers of his job and, like most cops, he knew he could be severely wounded or even killed someday. Yet he had never doubted that the sheriff's office and the county officials would look after him and his family if that ever occured.

That had *not* happened, and he knew someone had to be personally responsible for it. His gut instinct told him Sheriff Catlin was the culprit. If Catlin had put the word out to stay away from him, few would risk their jobs to visit or call him. They would bury their heads in the sand and hope no one noticed what cowards they were.

While working under this sheriff for the past few years, Matt had tried to distance himself from Catlin's questionable tactics and political priorities. He managed to concentrate on solving crimes, guiding his men and burying himself in the work of a detective. Maybe that had grated against Catlin's ego more than the man had let on, and he decided to attack him while he was so vulnerable. Matt intended to find out what the hell was going on behind the scenes. His old department was a gossipy group at best and word would eventually get back to him.

Since no one in his department was keeping him informed of anything regarding the fugitives, he and Cynthia tried to stay abreast of events by watching television and reading newspaper accounts. Dynamic scenes of confusion and desperation were being played out in the high desert back country, and Matt read how law enforcement agencies from four states had converged on Cortez, including five-hundred officers from sixty-four different agencies. Most of them had arrived unannounced, but all of them were there to help take down the killers of a fellow cop.

He was well aware of the unspoken code among police officers that called for the full fury of the law to come down hard on anyone who takes the life of a police officer, especially if it was in cold blood. The public might not always understand that, but it was this code that sent a signal to those who might think about killing a cop. It was a safety barrier between the law and those who would break the law.

When the officer had been killed on that bridge and law enforcement agencies from four states came to track down those guys, the message was:

41

"You don't kill one of ours and walk away. We'll hound you until we bring you down."

It had to be that way. Each time a cop finds himself alone out there, he needs to know and believe that dozens of other cops will come to his aide if he gets in a jam. But it should go beyond that. His fellow deputies and supervisors should have been there when they brought him into the hospital. They should be here now, letting him know what was going on to get those guys. Instead, they had turned their backs on him.

He now knew the stolen water truck had been taken from an oil field parking lot near Ignacio, Colorado. When the officer who had been killed spotted the truck and began following it, the driver of the truck had pulled over and stopped.

As the officer pulled up behind the truck, one of the three men had jumped out of the passenger's seat and ran toward the police car, firing a wild barrage of bullets straight into the windshield where the unsuspecting officer sat. The officer had died instantly, hit by nineteen shots from an automatic SKS rifle before he could even unbuckle his seat belt. It had been such a vicious and unexpected attack, he had not had a chance.

Witnesses identified twenty-six-year-old Jay Vista of Durango as the triggerman, and it was soon determined that his accomplices were twenty-six-year-old Dan Stone of Durango and thirty-year-old Alec Column of Dove Creek. Matt and Cynthia remembered the nurse at the hospital who had told them Column was her cousin.

Looking at their pictures, they didn't look all that different than dozens of other guys around the Cortez area. Vista was tall and lanky, with sandy-colored hair and beard. His face was long and narrow and he had round, puppy-dog eyes.

Alec Column was a large, robust guy with a round face and receding hairline. Dan Stone was fit and muscular with a strong face and burr haircut. None of these guys looked like crazy killers.

However, the trio were known in the Durango area as survivalists who nursed a growing hatred for all government and law enforcement agencies. They were now heavily armed and extremely dangerous with nothing to lose.

After encountering Matt and leaving him for dead, the fugitives had continued on their high-speed killing journey, racing toward U.S. 160 with four police cruisers hot on their tail. Barreling through a busy intersection, they had shot at a car and a garbage truck which in turn caused a major traffic jam and stopped the police cruisers dead.

The fugitives had quickly disappeared up McElmo Canyon, going deep into the canyonlands where thousands of twisted arroyos and hidden pockets in side canyons could easily provide shelter for them. The Navajos believe strong evil spirits reside in these canyonlands to this day and when Cynthia heard that, she commented dryly, "I guess they're just returning to their roots."

Roadblocks had been set up on Highway 666, causing huge traffic delays as all vehicles were stopped and searched by law officers in military gear armed with high-powered rifles. Seeing it later on television, Matt thought it looked more like a movie set filled with Black Hawk helicopters and hundreds of police officers than reality. Needless to say, people in all four states were glued to their television sets.

While Matt was being operated on, a park ranger near the Hovenweep National Park encountered a flatbed truck racing toward him and recognized it as the one described on the all-points bulletin. He wasn't about to take those guys on by himself, so he quickly steered his government car into a ditch and ducked on the floor for cover. As the truck sped by, bullets sprayed his car, the road and the ditch before the trio disappeared over a distant hill. Miraculously, the ranger wasn't hurt.

Officers had immediately converged on the area, but the fugitives were gone by the time they reached it. These guys were looking more and more like phantoms, appearing and disappearing at will. Less than an hour later, a deputy in Cross Canyon was seriously wounded by an unseen assailant, and when lawmen once again rushed to the site, they found the flatbed truck abandoned on a deadend road just across the Utah border. The fugitives were gone, yet officers found only *two* sets of footprints leading from the truck. Where was the third one?

After his operation, Matt had little to do but watch the latest about the manhunt. When news reporters were talking about the latest officer hurt by the fugitives, Cynthia brought up her feelings about the area directly around the Mesa Verde National Park, which was close to Hovenweep National Park.. The Mesa Verde ruins were near Cortez and had a dark, cruel history. She noted, "Whenever we go near there, I feel cold even if it's ninety degrees out."

They had both read about the Anasazi Indians who had once lived on that high mesa for six-hundred years. Then they had vanished, leaving behind pots sitting on cold ashes and clay dishes ready to be served. An entire civilization was gone, leaving no graves behind.

The popular series "The X-Files" filmed one segment in the Four Corners area. In one scene, a Native American was telling Fox Mulder about the Anasazi Indians and how they were really 'aliens' who had disappeared into the sky one day. Considering the unsettling feelings she had when in that area, Cynthia could almost believe the stories.

Their abandoned but finely crafted city was amazing with its hand-chipped, precisely fitted stones. Ladders which could be pulled up in case of danger reached rooms fifty feet above the main floors. The Anasazi people had built their homes to last, yet had left suddenly and it appeared they didn't stop to take anything with them. What had frightened them so badly?

.

Cynthia was sitting next to Matt's hospital bed as they talked about these mysteries when she said, "*Chindi*. That's the Navajo word for "evil spirit." The Navajos believe the Anasazi ran for their lives, but not even scientists can find any traces of battles. Now they have new evidence that the Anasazi had been enslaved by really evil neighboring Indians. They say there are signs of cannibalism."

She shivered. "Maybe that's why I feel so cold when I'm in the area. Maybe it's traces of this evil left over."

Matt raised his eyebrow. "Maybe."

She knew he didn't always understand her "sixth sense." "The Navajo people also tell stories about the area where that police officer was killed and where *you* were wounded. Hundreds have died there over the years, and they believe it's an ancient evil that can influence those who are susceptible to such things."

She looked at Matt. "I wonder if that evil force is controlling the three fugitives? That could explain why the police are having such a hard time catching them."

Matt shrugged his shoulders. "It can also mean that those guys are just knowledgeable enough to use the canyons and dry washes to their advantage. The creekbeds are lined with cottonwoods and thorny bushes that can conceal a man easily. A good survivalist could disappear without a trace."

Cynthia looked uncertain. "So you've never sensed anything strange in that area?"

"Let's just say I sometimes sense *something* is there, but I don't know what."

She took a deep breath, satisfied with his answer. "I've always felt better up in the high mountains than in the canyonlands. And another thing, why would someone name the highway south of Cortez Route 666?"

"That's a good question."

As a Christian, he had always wondered about that too, especially since the number 666 is depicted as the mark of the devil in the Bible. The narrow highway was two lanes all the way to Gallop, New Mexico and this made it difficult to pass slower vehicles, causing people to take chances. As a witness to this, flowers with markers could be seen here and there along the highway as a memorial to those who had been killed.

She cut into his thoughts. "Do you remember the last time we made the trip to Flagstaff and had to take Route 666?"

He nodded. It had been the middle of July, and temperatures were in the 100's. Hot winds were blowing straight off the desolate, crumbling mesas and were blasting their car with fine pebbles of dirt, rock and gravel. He'd been irritated at that, knowing the car's paint was taking a beating.

She continued, "The dust was so thick it was filling up the sky. Those large rock formations that looked like cathedrals rising up from the desert were encircled by the blowing dust which looked like fog circling around them. It was all pretty eerie."

"Yeah, it was. I remember one of the rock formations looked just like a ship with full-blown sailing masts."

"Right! The Navajos didn't want that highway built in the first place. That land is sacred to them." She stared at him, "Maybe they put a curse on it."

"It's hard to explain some things."

She was caught up in that scene from a year ago. "Even those giant electrical structures lined up across the hills looked like some kind of witchcraft symbols."

"Honey …"

"Do you remember I thought someone was watching us from the hills?"

He seemed surprised at her question. "Uh … no, I don't.."

"You blamed it on my sixth sense working overtime."

"I did?"

"You did. And now, just one year later, those same canyons are the focal point of one of the biggest manhunts the southwest has ever seen, and *you* were one of the casualties."

TEN

When Governor Romer declared to the press that he wanted Colorado to get a better handle on all militia groups operating within the western states, the locals shook their heads and wondered how the heck he was going to accomplish that. They were aware of how secretive those groups were, and even if one of them was helping the fugitives, how would the Governor prove it? So far, the cops hadn't come close to capturing those three guys..

Then the whole situation worsened when too many people became involved. Radio communications were insufficient, making the relay of information poor. As law enforcement agencies continued hunting the fugitives in the hot, canyon-choked land, they often felt they were being hunted themselves. This was the fugitives' backyard, and they could be behind a rock or in a hidden crevice and never be seen before it was too late.

The police now held more information on the fugitives. Besides having anti-government views, Alec Column was known as an extreme racist who was a member of a local "patriot group." This local group was rumored to be affiliated with a nationwide militia group who identified themselves as a "Christian religion" with viciously racist and anti-Semitic views. This "religion" believed Jews were satanic and blacks less than human. Since the Oklahoma bombing, they had become more outspoken and violent.

Police obtained search warrants and found maps of the area, lists of large quantities of food supplies, plans about chemical warfare, some pipe bombs, several guns and grenades among the fugitives' personal effects. What had they been planning when they began stockpiling all those items? If they had been successful in their plans, it was evident they had formulated a scheme that would allow them to stay hidden for a long time.

The fugitives knew how to walk on the sides of their feet to hide tracks and could step on brush in such a way that it wouldn't be flattened. They had evidently hopped from rock to rock instead of walking in the dirt. Therefore, it was decided that Navajo trackers might be the lawmen's best bet in finding these guys. Their trackers could also look at a blade of grass or overturned rock or a snapped twig and tell what or who had gone that way. Yet the fugitives remained free.

* * *

During the massive manhunt, reporters began calling Matt, asking for interviews. He gave one interview after his first week in the hospital, but tried limiting his answers to just his part in the shootings.

A week after Matt had been shot, a sniper's bullet seriously wounded a San Juan County sheriff's deputy near Bluff, Utah. The deputy had been shot on the bank of the San Juan River near the small colorful artists' colony of approximately three-hundred people. He had climbed onto a ridge to survey the area when three shots rang out, and he was hit twice, once in the back and once in the shoulder.

SWAT teams, dog teams and helicopters swarmed the area within minutes of the shooting. Since the south side of the San Juan River marks the northern boundary of the Navajo Reservation, Navajo police were staked out there. By mid-afternoon, Bluff had been sealed off from the public and the town had been evacuated.

Many residents of this tiny town felt a total evacuation wasn't necessary, and that it wouldn't be happening if a cop hadn't been killed. Very independent people lived in this isolated area of Utah and they believed they could take care of themselves. A lot of them were sympathetic to the fugitives and may even have helped them, which bothered Matt. Maybe it all looked like an exciting game to them, but those guys were cold killers and needed to be stopped.

Just as night began to fall, a body was discovered in a campground five miles east of Bluff. Dan Stone, wearing body armor, camouflage, a helmet and several pipe bombs, was a suspected suicide. However, no sign of the other two fugitives were found. They were either holed up somewhere, or they had escaped the area.

Matt found himself questioning the 'suicide' verdict. It wouldn't surprise him if Vista and Column had decided to get rid of Stone before they abandoned the truck. That would account for finding only two men's footprints near the abandoned truck of the three men.

Matt believed Dan Stone might be the least violent of the trio. Maybe Stone had wanted out, and they had shot him execution-style; up close and personal.

The next day the Denver Post headlines read: "PARANOIA!" One resident near Bluff, Utah was quoted as saying, "If I see a shadow, I shoot it!"

The reporter wrote that Governor Romer was worried and had made the decision to bring in the Colorado National Guard. Matt shook his head. *More law enforcement agencies in an area already deluged with them.*

* * *

While staying with Matt in the hospital, Cynthia used some of her spare time to read up on different militia groups and was surprised to find out how well organized they actually were. She had pictured groups of uneducated men who blamed the world for their shortcomings. She discovered they had their own Internet pages and intelligence networks, and their main targets seemed to be law enforcement and military personnel. Her mind began racing. *They thought they had killed Matt. What if they decide to send someone to finish the job? Not only kill Matt, but also other officers who could identify them.*

She knew the sheriff's office could not be counted on to protect her husband once he returned home and, at this point, she had no confidence in their abilities anyway. Three men against hundreds of police and yet no arrests had been made. According to the papers, the one fugitive had killed himself even though Matt wasn't in total agreement with that finding. She knew the terrain was aiding the two remaining fugitives and hindering the lawmen, but it was frustrating. She also now believed that a local militia group *was* helping the killers to hide.

When fear raises its ugly head, it can produce a lot of uncertainties. She was dealing with situations over which she had no control, and she wasn't sure what or who to believe. Matt was confident the shooting wasn't personal. Maybe it wasn't at the time, but what about now? These guys were on the run now, and they would never be able to come back to the life they had once known.

Matt's and her life had also been changed forever through no choice of their own, and she knew it was going to take a lot of perseverance and faith to get through the next few months.

ELEVEN

Since Matt was still in the hospital when the slain officer's funeral was held, the hospital staff arranged for an ambulance to take him and Cynthia to the graveside service.

Governor Romer spoke at the funeral where two-thousand people attended while bagpipes played "Amazing Grace." The officer's casket was taken by a horse-drawn hearse to the cemetery, followed by three-hundred police cruisers, rescue vehicles and families as bagpipes played. Hundreds of citizens and visitors lined the streets in respect for the officer and his family.

A cop had died in the line of duty and law enforcement from all four states of the Four Corners region were there to honor their fallen comrade. They all came in uniform.

While the ambulance that was carrying Matt and Cynthia made its way slowly down the road leading into the cemetery, Matt saw how each side of the road was lined with officers. As though being given an unseen signal, one officer after the other saluted him as the ambulance passed by.

It caught him by surprise, and he found himself moved to tears at their display of respect for him during this sad day. Cynthia's eyes were also brimming with tears as she tightly clasped his hand. Neither of them spoke.

The driver parked the ambulance in a roped-off section where Matt could view the casket as guns were fired in the slain officer's honor. Once the ceremony was over, news reporters rushed over to Matt's ambulance in order to get a picture of him, but his nurse blocked their view.

She told the reporters, "Thank you for your concern, but Detective Nelson is still too weak for interviews."

Once they returned to the hospital, Matt found himself filled with conflicting emotions. He was thankful he hadn't died, but he was now looking at a future that was anything but certain. Pain dominated his life and the moment he was wheeled into his room, he had to ask for medication to take off the edge.

Weakened by the trip to the grave site, he now felt totally exhausted. The nurse who had accompanied them in the ambulance helped him get back in bed, where he stretched out as best as he could. Cynthia sat down on the chair next to him, filled with her own uncertainties. Today had brought everything into sharp focus, and she knew she had to be ready for whatever the future might bring.

She had been trying to keep her wavering emotions under control and stay strong for Matt, but there was this trepidation building in her. Once Matt returned home, their families would only be able to help so much; the rest of the time they would be on their own.

Glancing at her husband, she saw the medicine was finally taking affect and his whole body was loosening up and relaxing as he sunk deeper into his pillow. Just as his eyes closed, a nurse walked in and said, "Mr. Nelson, I hope I'm not disturbing you, but you have some visitors I think you might want to see. A young boy and girl, and their parents. They said they want to thank you."

Matt shook himself awake, his eyes still groggy. "Oh. Uh, sure. Bring them in."

A girl and boy, maybe ten and eleven years old, entered the room followed by a couple in their thirties. The woman smiled and said, "Detective Nelson, this is Ashley and Adam. You saved their lives when you took on those killers all by yourself. When you put yourself in the line of fire, you gave our children a chance to jump off their bikes and lie on the ground. We wanted to come and say thank you in person."

Matt smiled as he looked over at two children standing by the door. "So you're the ones I saw on the bikes. Sorry I didn't have time to warn you, but I saw those guys coming straight toward you and I needed to try and stop them."

Ashley smiled shyly. "We were really scared."

Adam spoke up, "Yeah, and then we saw them shoot you! We thought you were dead!"

Matt nodded, "It was a close call."

The father stepped forward and extended his hand to Matt. "I'd like to personally thank you, Detective Nelson. We will always be grateful for what you did ... for putting yourself out there like that."

Matt shook the man's extended hand and answered, "I'm glad they're okay."

They saw how tired he was, so they didn't stay long. As they were leaving, the woman turned to look at him and said, "We're praying for you, Detective Nelson. We hope that you make a full recovery."

Matt felt the effect of the medicine taking over and knew he couldn't stay awake much longer. He smiled. "Thanks. I appreciate that."

As they disappeared from sight, Matt looked at Cynthia, his eyes already half-closing, and said, "I forgot to tell you about them. They were another reason I had to try and stop those guys. Those kids had no idea what was coming their way."

Cynthia nodded and reached out to squeeze his hand. She knew Matt would have had no other choice when he saw two kids on their bikes. He did what he had to do.

* * *

Two weeks after the shooting

The doctor decided Matt was strong enough to begin more intense physical therapy and transferred him to the rehabilitation section of the hospital. Knowing he had some rough times ahead, Matt decided to stay secluded from the press and the curious because he was going to need every bit of strength he could muster to get back on his feet. The first week in therapy was pretty discouraging. He was so weak he could barely stand up and was unable to put any weight on his wounded leg. Whenever he tried to, the pain was so excruciating he would almost pass out.

However, through sheer willpower, he was able to walk a few steps by the second week. He would listen to what the therapist said, then proceed to go further. If Cynthia caught him doing this, he would promise to take it easier, but as soon as she left, he would once more push himself. He was going to walk again; then he was going to run!

The big day finally arrived when the doctor said he could go home. After signing all the paperwork and being presented with an assortment of prescriptions, the nurse arrived to wheel him out of the hospital. Matt couldn't contain the big grin that crept across his face. It was Liberation Day, and Cynthia had brought his son, Josh, to the hospital to escort him home.

His brother, Monroe, and his sister-in-law were back at the house preparing for his arrival. Cynthia's mother was cooking his coming-home dinner, and he couldn't get out of that hospital fast enough. He was appreciative of the great care he had received from the staff, but he missed his real life.

A handicapped van transported him home, while Cynthia and Josh followed in the Jeep. His mother and father lived in Utah and since they had already visited him when he had first been hurt, they had called earlier to congratulate him on going home and said they would be seeing him soon.

The dinner was ready when they pulled into their driveway. As everyone sat down to eat, Matt bowed his head and said a prayer, thanking God for the miracle of coming home again and for the happiness he felt as he sat surrounded by those he loved most in the world.

His brother then lifted his wine glass and toasted Matt, saying, "To my brother, who is now on his way to becoming the second trooper to grace our family."

Everyone joined in the toast, and Matt found himself looking around the table at his family. His heart was filled to bursting. He was struck with just how important life with your family can be and how close he had come to losing it all. He would never take anything for granted again.

That night as he lie in his own bed for the first time in weeks, Cynthia carefully snuggled against him, mindful of his wounds. "Is this okay, Honey? I'm not hurting you, am I?"

He felt his eyes closing, but he struggled to keep them open. "No. Stay right where you are. It feels good."

"You're home now, Matt. Things are going to get better and better."

"I know. It won't be easy, but right now I couldn't be happier."

He had taken his pills shortly before going to bed and as much as he wanted to stay awake, he soon faded into a dreamless sleep.

Cynthia realized the day had been exhausting for Matt, but as she looked at his face, now relaxed in sleep, her heart slowed down. Her husband was home where he belonged. She knew he would heal faster in his own home, but in the meantime, she needed to mentally prepare herself for the coming weeks. It would be harder than anything she'd ever done before, but she knew she could do it.

She leaned over and gently kissed his face, then laid back down and closed her eyes. They were going to make it through this life-altering adversity, and they were going to be stronger and closer for it.

TWELVE

On Matt's second day home, two deputies from the sheriff's office unexpectedly stopped by the house. Matt's pleasure at seeing them soon faded as the pair acted uncomfortable and didn't stay long. After that day, all visits stopped.

The disappointment he felt frustrated and hurt him, but he knew he had to put those issues in perspective. He was embroiled in one of the biggest battles of his life, and it was going to take every bit of his strength just to continue the painful and often torturous therapies.

Cynthia was driving him to and from the hospital four times a week for sessions, then he would continue with the therapy at home. She had taken over the role of his nurse, cleaning his wounds to prevent infection, helping him in and out of bed and the bathtub and aiding him in dressing.

She didn't complain, but he knew it really got to her at times. As he witnessed her struggling to care for him twenty-four hours a day, he found himself getting even more angry at his department. They had not only turned their backs on him, but also on his family.

During the next few weeks, a caring neighbor helped stack their wood and a community effort produced special Tee shirts referencing the shootings and manhunt. Proceeds from their sale were sent to the slain officer's home, to the now-recovered Officer Pope and to Matt. Those acts of kindness really touched him. He had joked with one of the ladies who brought a check to him, saying, "I didn't know you liked cops so much. I thought it was just firemen."

The lady had laughed heartily, and said, "We like you too, Matt."

His own department remained silent.

As the long days stretched on, Matt worked hard and graduated from a wheelchair to crutches. He was bubbling with excitement when he took his first careful steps. By the end of the day, he was aching so bad he felt like an eighty-year-old man.

The next morning he could barely move, and Cynthia had to help him out of bed. Until he had a hot bath, each move he made was excruciating. Damn, he hated being this helpless! Seeing Cynthia laboring to assist him was almost too much to take, but she would get upset whenever he suggested they hire an aide until he was better.

She promised she would tell him if she couldn't handle some things, and she steadfastly continued to encourage and care for him. They were both aware that whenever one member of a family experiences a life-changing event, it affects the whole family. It could either make or break a marriage too. He and Cynthia were learning to cope with the changes, but it was difficult.

While he was struggling around the house on crutches, his doctors were trying to prepare him for the possibility of never being able to walk without a severe limp. It had alarmed him to hear those words, but he steeled himself, determined he was going to prove them wrong. There was no way he was going to accept that prognosis. He couldn't and he wouldn't.

For part of his home therapy, he had to place his knee in a special device for several hours a day to get it to bend a small amount. Day and night, he would slowly crank the device up further to keep his knee limber. It hurt like hell, and there were times he felt like he might pass out, but he kept pushing himself well beyond what he was told.

When his doctor told him they needed to graft more skin onto his left arm, he knew it would set him back. It was discouraging, but it had to be done if he was going to use that arm again. Following the operation, they put his arm in a cast that extended straight out from his shoulder. The doctor patiently explained to him that the cast was necessary to prevent scar tissue from forming, which could cause his arm to tighten into a permanent curl. Not a pleasant thought.

After one day in the confining cast, he wanted to yell out against what life had handed him. He thought he was encumbered before; now he couldn't even button his shirt or tie his own shoelaces without help from Cynthia. As each day passed, he found himself becoming more and more despondent no matter how much he fought against it.

Along with the cast on his arm, he was also wearing a brace attached just below his knee by a rod and two bolts that had been screwed directly into the bone. Amazingly, they didn't hurt. Metal wire hoops were also inserted into his leg for stability, and now his son was comparing him to the bionic man. He wished he did have bionic powers because he was shuffling around the house like great-grandpa Nelson.

Matt had always taken his physical strength for granted, and it was disconcerting to glimpse his reflection in the patio glass door as he hobbled past it. With the cast sticking straight out in front of him and the rod and bolts attached to his leg reflecting the afternoon sun, he felt more like a robot than a bionic man.

Forensics had identified the bullet that smashed through his knee as an SKS armored bullet. His arm had been hit by a 308 assault bullet, but both were deadly and had done massive injury to his limbs. Bullet fragments that looked like grains of sand remained imbedded in his arm and, over time, they began inching their way out through his skin, much to Cynthia's dismay.

An X-ray of his knee showed where the copper-jacketed bullet was still lodged in the bone. It had splintered and looked like corn flakes scattered throughout the inside of his knee. He would carry those souvenirs around forever.

The doctor wouldn't allow him to use crutches while his arm was in the cast, which forced him to hop around on his good leg or use a wheelchair when he got too fatigued. During the ensuing weeks, Matt experienced some pretty bad days. He found himself staring out the window at people walking by, going about their normal lives, and a feeling of despair would encompass him. He had never felt that way before in his life, and it was weighing heavily on his psyche.

Always appreciative of everything Cynthia was doing for him, he still hated being so dependent on her. In their marriage, they had always prided themselves on being equal partners; now he wasn't able to do his part. It was killing him inside and he knew Cynthia was having a harder time dealing with his mental state than his physical one..

Depression set in and there were days when he didn't want to get up and face another one. However, Cynthia fought for him. She would sit next to him and start talking. She would remind him of his goal to attend the Academy and how he could do anything he set his mind to. She had never seen him turn his back on a challenge, and he knew she was banking on that same resoluteness to see himself through this too.

Thank God for his wife.

Over time, friends stopped coming over to help with chores and he couldn't depend on his parents because they lived out of state. Monroe, his older brother who was with the state patrol, helped whenever he could, but he was stationed in Denver

He hated to see Cynthia struggling to push their heavy gasoline lawn mower. They had a large yard and she mowed it each week, plus she kept the house up and catered to him. When Matt heard about the aid that had been ongoing for the officer's family who had been killed, it bothered him. He agreed that the community *should* help them and he applauded their kind efforts. However, it would have been nice if someone had offered a little help to them while he was still looking like a Star Wars robot.

* * *

Days turned into weeks and everything settled down into a routine of therapies and doctor appointments. Matt and Cynthia tried to make some time for themselves, but they were both so exhausted at the end of each day they would just go to bed and fall into a deep sleep. Now that he was beyond the acute medical stage, he was realizing how difficult it was to allow himself the luxury of relaxation. Time was against him, so he didn't dare slow down.

Whenever he became too frustrated from the pressures of his therapies and dealing with the all-encompassing pain, he would often get a warm, comforting feeling that seemed to fold around him like a blanket. Cynthia told him it was God's angels giving him a helping hand, so he'd pick himself up and start again. There was no way he was going to let destructive emotions control him while he was in the biggest battle of his life.

It had now been a couple of months since the shooting, and Cynthia was beginning to worry about how they were going to make ends meet while he was in rehabilitation. She finally broached the subject with him. "Why haven't you received a check from the sheriff's office yet, Matt? They told you you're still on their payroll, but what do they mean by that? Since they don't even come by to see how you're doing, I don't have a lot of confidence in their sense of fair play."

He knew she was right, and he immediately initiated a call to the sheriff's Personnel Department. The switchboard operator transferred him to a lady in bookkeeping who explained that he would soon be receiving Workers' Compensation, and that the County would start using up his accumulated sick leave hours from the past nine years.

This was how he would be "paid" while healing.

When he hung up, it hit him hard when he realized that once his sick time was used up, he might have to return to work at the sheriff's office until he was strong enough to go to the State Patrol. Since his old department wasn't even talking to him, there wouldn't be any welcome mats laid out for his return.

As the weeks slowly rolled by, he began feeling more and more uncertain about his likelihood of making the Academy. For all intents and purposes, he was now categorized as physically disabled.

When the arm cast and leg hardware were finally removed, it wasn't a big moment where he took off and walked. Each move he made still brought jolts of pain to his injured limbs, but he was alive. He still had two arms and two legs, and deep in his soul, he knew God had a specific plan for him. He was clinging to the hope that the plan would include attending the academy, so he kept pushing himself to the limit.

Cynthia was keeping a critical eye on him, and if she noticed that the strain of what he was trying to accomplish was wearing him down, she would remind him to slow down and stay focused.

Matt thought of how people in the Orient walked over red hot coals without injuring themselves. It had to do with the power of faith. A verse in the Bible states that if you want a mountain taken up and cast into the sea, you must believe it can happen.

Well, the mountain's in my way, Lord,, and I want it thrown into the sea.

Three months after the shooting
••

By August, he amazed everyone when he started walking with just the aid of a cane. Granted, he still had a bad limp, but damn, it felt good to walk uninhibited by crutches and braces. Encouraged by his accomplishments, Matt renewed his efforts to go farther and faster. *The mountain was still in his way, but it didn't look so big now.*

By September, the cane was gone and he was walking on his own! Though a visible limp remained, his dream of attending the academy was back in his head again, and now he had to *run*.

Those who sincerely cared for him wanted the best for him, but only Cynthia believed it was truly possible. Using a treadmill, he began by walking, then building up to a slow jog. He was unable to run on hard ground yet, but he was happy with the small gains he was making each day.

He knew how limited his employment options would be unless he could attend the Academy. His personal rehabilitation had been formidable and exhausting, accompanied by oppressive pain, but the black tunnel now had a light at the end of it. He believed he had a good chance of making it.

* * *

A week later, Matt was at home doing his daily exercises when the phone rang. To his surprise, it was Tom Wahl, a detective at the sheriff's office. They chatted for a few minutes, and Tom finally asked, "Hey, heard anything from the State Patrol?"

Matt hesitated, suddenly knowing what the phone call was all about. Swallowing hard, he said, "I'm waiting to see how things go."

"Yeah? So I hear you're walking without a cane now. Shouldn't be too long, right?"

Matt decided it was time to say what was on his mind. "You know, it'd be nice to have a few of the guys from my old department stop by the house now and then. You could see for yourself what progress I'm making."

Tom laughed self-consciously. "Hey, as soon as this manhunt eases up, we'll do that."

"Sure."

"Well, guess I'd better get back to work. Talk to you later."

"The manhunt … right?"

"What? Oh! Yeah, right."

When Tom hung up, Matt felt the anger rising in him again. Didn't they know how obvious they were? He'd like to believe they were just trying to wipe out whatever guilt feelings they might have had for turning their backs on him while he was fighting to survive, but he knew they didn't give a damn about him or his family. The only concern they had was to assure themselves he was gone permanently. He didn't care about the sheriff, but he wished he understood why his fellow deputies had turned against him.

60

He could only surmise that everything was coming from the perverse mind of Sheriff Catlin. Thank God for the continuing phone calls from the highway patrol personnel office in Denver asking about his progress. They said they wanted him in the next Academy, and they meant it.

He hated to think he still might have to go back to the sheriff's office, if only on a temporary basis, but it could happen. He was physically pushing himself as much as he dared. Any more and he took the chance of damaging what the doctors had so painstakingly pieced together three months ago. He would just proceed with his therapy and keep his faith that things would work out for the good.

THIRTEEN

While Matt was exerting all of his energy in getting back to a fit physical condition, the search for the fugitives had ground to a slow crawl. The sheriff's office was making sure he wasn't privy to anything regarding the ongoing investigation, so he kept himself informed the same way he had from the beginning … through the newspapers, television and other law agencies.

One of his primary questions remained unsolved. Who had driven the three fugitives to the site of the large water truck? That truck had evidently been extremely important to their plans, especially considering the arsenal they took along to protect it.

If the officer who had been killed had not spotted them, what would they have done with it? They knew the killing of that officer would bring every cop in the area down on them. Since they couldn't escape while still driving the big clumsy water truck, they had abandoned the very thing that had caused this whole mess and hijacked the flatbed truck they were driving when they faced him.

After shooting him, they had eluded the police and headed toward a spot that may have been pre-planned, where they abandoned the flatbed and took off on foot into the canyonlands. Had someone picked them up at a pre-arranged place? Whatever happened, they were long gone and Matt suspected the two remaining guys were receiving help from their militia buddies.

He found it ironic that public interest had continued over his involvement in the shootings. People from "America's Most Wanted" and "Unsolved Mysteries" had called for interviews. Re-enactments of how he was wounded were filmed on location, and a friend of his wife's was hired to portray him in the short film. They showed how he tried to stop three heavily-armed killers by himself and ended up fighting for his life. Suddenly he found himself somewhat of a hero, which is the last thing he considered himself to be. He had been doing his job, plain and simple.

When related stories appeared regarding his battle to overcome his wounds, he began receiving caring letters from people in Colorado and other states. He was grateful for the public's ongoing interest in him, and it was gratifying to have strangers rooting for him to get well enough to attend the academy.

Throughout the blitz of narratives regarding Matt's part in the manhunt, there was an ominous silence from the sheriff's domain. Word soon trickled back to him that the sheriff was not real thrilled with the publicity that was keeping Matt in the news. That didn't surprise Matt, considering Catlin's compulsion to be in the spotlight himself.

A few weeks earlier, Sheriff Catlin had publicly announced he was taking an early retirement. When Matt had first heard the sheriff was backing Juan Sanchez to replace him in November, his antenna went up. Why Sanchez? The guy had no understanding of budgets or public relations, and was known for making more than a few gaffes. His background in administration and leadership was pretty much nonexistent. Of course, that could describe Catlin as well.

Forcing himself to think optimistically, Matt switched gears and gave some thought to Catlin choosing Sanchez because of a potential influence within the Hispanic community of the area. Whenever a group of ethnic people live in an oppressive state as they do in the Four Corners area, it would be good to have someone come forward to represent their interests. *No.* He couldn't see Sanchez in that role. So Catlin had to have another reason for bringing Sanchez in, then backing him for sheriff.

When he went to therapy at the hospital that afternoon, he ran into a friend, Wyatt Camry, who enthusiastically shook his hand and exclaimed. "Hey, Matt! You're lookin' a lot better than the last time I saw you. I guess you're gonna' make it after all."

Matt grinned. "Some days I think I am, and other days, I don't give a damn if I do or don't."

Wyatt laughed. "Understood. Hey, did you hear Tom Hill is gonna' run against Sanchez for sheriff?"

Matt was surprised. "No."

Tom was a former detective with the sheriff's office prior to Catlin being elected. He had also been the one who had personally trained Matt when he originally joined the department. Tom was an honest man who had gone on to college to get a degree in business and now had an extensive administrative background.

Wyatt asked, "Wasn't Tom the one who originally trained you at the sheriff's office?"

"He was. That was nine years ago. He'd be a good person for sheriff, especially with his background."

Wyatt chuckled. "Don't let Sheriff Catlin hear you say that."

Matt shrugged his shoulders. "I'd say it to his face."

Wyatt knew the reasons Matt had quit. "Yeah. I didn't think you'd be votin' for Sanchez."

"I would if I thought he was the best man for the job. I just think Tom has better qualifications."

Wyatt nodded. "Yeah, he probably does, but with Catlin campaigning for Sanchez, Tom will have an uphill battle."

"I think you're right. Well, I've got more important things to do right now than worry about who's going to be the next sheriff. It's good to see you, Wyatt. Come on out to the house some day. Cynthia and I would like that."

Wyatt smiled. "I'll do that. You take care."

Since everyone who worked for Sheriff Catlin was considered under the "umbrella" of the office, Matt knew they would all campaign for Sanchez. It had never been wise to show signs of individualism there and before Matt had quit, he found himself alone whenever he stood up for his men. That had landed him on the sheriff's "list" more than once, which was probably one of the reason Catlin didn't want him around. Sanchez was evidently more of a "yes" man.

Matt had no idea that his comments to Wyatt that day would get back to Catlin and that the election would turn the whole sheriff's office against him. He didn't believe Wyatt had said anything to the sheriff, but he may have told someone who did.

FOURTEEN

Four months after the shooting

....

Matt had to undergo a second surgery on his knee, which once again set him back in his exercise program. Frustrated, he was recuperating at home when he opened the local newspaper and read about his "demotion" in the mid-section of the paper.

What the heck was this all about?

Though he had already resigned, he was still on the sheriff's payroll because he hadn't shirked his duty that last day with them. He was very aware of how people would react when they read about his demotion in a public newspaper; they would assume he had screwed up in some way. Why else a demotion?

What purpose did Sheriff Catlin have for doing this when he damned well knew the reason he couldn't work at this point? It had to be to discredit him, but why?

He grabbed the phone and demanded to speak to Sheriff Catlin. Much to his surprise, the man himself got on the line. "Hello, Matt. What can I do for you?"

This was also the first time they had talked since the shooting. He decided to get right to the point. "What the hell is going on? What's this crap in the paper about me being demoted?"

The sheriff cleared his throat. "Calm down, Matt. After all, it *was* your last day on the job when you got shot. If you decide you need to stay with our department for now … you know, because of your wounds and all, then you have to understand you've been replaced by Detective Groggin."

"Yes, I understood that when I quit, but why would you put this in the paper when you know exactly why I'm not working?"

"Tell you what … why don't you come into the office, and we'll get this straightened out."

"Just tell me when."

* * *

After the second operation on his knee, Matt was required to have moderate therapy at the hospital and, after his conversation with the sheriff, Cynthia drove him over for his daily treatment.

He was just finishing his last set of leg exercises when he was approached by a reporter from a television station in Farmington, New Mexico. Matt figured the reporter was there as a follow-up to interviews he had given before. After the intense media attention of the past month, Matt felt pretty much at ease with reporters.

True to form, the reporter began by asking him how the therapies were going, but then he surprised Matt. "I read in the paper about you being demoted. Did you know that was going to happen?"

Matt shook his head. "Nope."

"So the first you knew about your demotion was through the newspaper?"

"That's right."

"Since the last thing you did with the sheriff's office was to try and stop three killers, for which you almost died, I'm not understanding the reason for a demotion."

"I'm still out on disability, so I'm not sure either."

"They can't demote you for that reason."

Matt shrugged his shoulders. "You'll have to ask the sheriff about that."

"I will."

The reporter waylaid Sheriff Catlin outside his office later that day. With cameras rolling, he asked the sheriff, "Is it true that an article in the newspaper is how Detective Matt Nelson, who is still recovering from his wounds inflicted during the manhunt when he faced three killers all alone, learned he had been demoted? And that he has no idea why he was demoted since he is still on disability?"

Caught off guard, Sheriff Catlin turned red and mumbled, "I wasn't aware of a demotion."

The reporter took out the clipped article and said, "Here it is. Straight from your office. So, this is how Matt Nelson found out he has been demoted, correct? Any comment as to why?"

The sheriff brusquely brushed by him and quickly scooted behind the steering wheel of his car, slamming the door in the reporter's face.

When Cynthia and Matt watched the news that evening, they were both surprised and elated. Cynthia exclaimed, "Look at Catlin's face, Honey! He looks like he's been caught with his pants down!"

She said this in her best Texas drawl, and Matt found himself chuckling. "I don't think this is going to earn me any brownie points with him."

Cynthia grinned. "Who cares? Maybe the people in town will start to see what a fraud Catlin is."

Matt sobered. "Don't count on it."

Staring at the television set, he shook his head. "God, the man sure knows how to lie. As though anyone would believe the sheriff himself doesn't know and approve every demotion that comes across his desk. Who does he think he's fooling?"

Cynthia shook her head. "He doesn't care if people believe him or not. He's the 'King,' Honey. He's hand-picked his successor and you're in his way for some reason."

* * *

Cynthia drove Matt to the sheriff's office the next morning and, because of the latest operation, he was once more on crutches. As he walked into the main entrance, a young woman stopped him and asked, "Excuse me. Are you Mr. Nelson?"

"Yes."

She smiled nervously. "Let me tell them you're here."

She was soon leading him back to Undersheriff Warner's office, where both Warner and Detective Sanchez were waiting for him. Sheriff Catlin was nowhere to be seen, and Matt knew why. He wouldn't want to show his face after that news story last night on television.

They shook hands and Warner asked, "So Matt … how's the rehab goin'?"

Matt raised his eyebrow. "If you're asking how I'm doing, I think I would have appreciated the question back on May 29th more than I do now."

Warner and Sanchez looked at each other, and Sanchez replied, "We've been kept informed about your progress, but we've been pretty busy with this damned manhunt, Matt. You know how that goes."

Matt nodded. "Yeah. So, what's this I read in the newspaper about being demoted? I mean, since Sheriff Catlin's not here to explain."

Warner shrugged his shoulders. "Sorry, Matt, but you officially quit, and we gave your supervisory position to Sergeant. Groggin. We only have room for one supervisor."

"As I told Sheriff Catlin, I knew my position was being reassigned when I turned in my resignation. However, since I'm still technically on the payroll, I'd like a reason for this demotion. Also, why would you demote me and put it in the newspaper for the whole town to read? What was the purpose of that?"

Sanchez cleared his throat. "As I said, we can't have two people with the same title, and after all, you had quit."

Matt stared at the former patrol sergeant. "And as I said … I understand that. What I don't understand is demoting me publicly."

Sanchez frowned. "Actually, we can choose how to demote you in any way we want. If you decide you want to remain on the payroll once you're on your feet again, we'll put you where *we* think you'll fit in."

Matt nodded. "Which is real similar to when the sheriff gave that promotion to you, isn't it, Juan? He re-hired you and tells me to train you. Which is the real reason I quit, and you know it."

Sanchez looked up, but said nothing.

Matt turned and maneuvered his crutches through the door and toward the door. Outside, he put his face up toward the sunshine. The dark shadows from within the sheriff's office disappeared, and he adjusted his crutches as he walked to his car.

Cynthia took one look at his face and knew he was angry. As he opened the passenger door and scooted in, placing his crutches in the back, she asked, "How did it go?"

Matt met her eyes. "I knew what I was walking into. I mean, what did I expect?"

Cynthia looked at him in concern. "What did they say?"

"That it was their choice to put it in the paper. They opted to not give me a real reason, but it's obvious they wanted to cast doubts on my reputation. I'm just trying to figure out why it's so damned important to discredit me."

Cynthia reached over and took his hand. "Let it go, Matt. They can't discredit you with your record. It's without a blemish."

"But will the public know the truth of what's going on?"

She understood that he not only needed his physical strength to continue his rehab, but his mind needed to be clear in order to keep his spirits up. Those jerks at the sheriff's office didn't realize what an exceptional, honest and caring cop Matt was and always had been. Or maybe they did, and that was part of the problem.

As she pulled out of the parking lot, she glanced over at the grim expression on Matt's face and knew that look. He would stand up for what he believed in even if he was on crutches or in a wheelchair.

FIFTEEN

One week later, the Purple Heart was presented to Matt in a special ceremony. attended by County Administrators, the mayor and law enforcement officials. The local papers ran the story with a picture of Detective Juan Sanchez standing next to Matt, who was still using his crutches. Sanchez had made sure he was in a position to get his picture taken next to Matt. Sure, now that the guy was running for sheriff, Matt knew he wanted to look good in the public eye.

Matt appreciated the support of the public and was gracious in accepting the medal. However, he perceived from the fake smile on Sanchez's face that it was costing him to be nice.

Rumors were already circulating that certain promises had been made *before* Catlin hired Sanchez back and gave him the position promised Matt. Evidently Sheriff Catlin didn't want to retire completely. He wanted Sanchez to assure him a specific job in return for his political backing. When Sanchez had reputedly agreed, Catlin made room to hire him back not just as a deputy, but as a supervisor.

Sanchez didn't have the credentials and background for the position of head of detectives and patrol, but something that trivial wouldn't have stopped Catlin. He needed to get Matt out of the picture in order for all his plans to work, so he re-hired Sanchez and gave him the promotion Matt had been expecting. Catlin knew it would force Matt to make a decision to stay or quit. Matt could just imagine how jubilant everyone must have been when he turned in his resignation. They didn't care where he went; they just wanted him gone.

Matt had also heard through the grapevine that Sheriff Catlin had promised Deputy Pope a promotion if he helped get Sanchez elected. In summary, Catlin and Sanchez were making promises to lots of people in order to get the votes. Sanchez would owe people if he got in. Matt knew how the game worked, but it had always rubbed him the wrong way.

He could just imagine what thoughts went through their minds when the shootings occurred on Matt's last day with them. He could also visualize the hurried meetings to put their heads together and decide how Matt's hospitalization would effect their plans. Since he had still been on the sheriff's payroll when he was wounded, they knew he would be their responsibility until he could physically move on. *If* he was able to move on.

One officer from the city police department had visited Matt at home following the Purple Heart ceremony. He informed Matt that a meeting *had* been called between Sheriff Catlin and Juan Sanchez after they had been advised that Matt might lose his arm and leg.

The officer shook his head. "They were worried about public opinion if you were permanently handicapped. The last thing they wanted was to have you back in the department with a lot of public sympathy comin' your way."

Matt raised his eyebrow. "So that's the reason no one from administration came to visit me in the hospital?"

"I guess that's one of the reasons. I don't think Sanchez likes the attention you've been gettin' from the press either. He wants to use the publicity from this manhunt to lock in his bid for sheriff. You know, playin' the hero and all."

Matt was angry. "I was fighting for my life, and all he was worrying about was getting votes?"

His friend shrugged his shoulders. "You know how that political bullshit is played, Matt. A lot of us figure that's the reason for the public demotion. Make it look like you'd done something wrong, though all you did was quit."

At least he now had a better handle on what was happening with Catlin and Sanchez. Knowing what he was up against should give him a better chance at handling things in the future. Or so he thought.

* * *

Nothing eventful happened during the two weeks subsequent to the Purple Heart being awarded to Matt. Then more rumors began circulating back to him. Someone in the sheriff's office began spreading the word within the department that since Matt had 'chosen' to quit, he was to be left alone. *Hadn't they already done a good job of that?* He also thought it was pretty ironic since Sanchez himself had quit and then been re-hired by the sheriff.

It really bugged him when he heard that personal friends and acquaintances from other law enforcement agencies were also advised to keep their distance, and he realized the sheriff was trying to isolate him from those who might support him.. To everyone's credit, they told the sheriff's cronies that they would talk to anyone they wanted to.

It came as no shock to Matt when he heard that everyone who worked for the sheriff had agreed to line up behind Sanchez. All cowards, they put their careers first, not realizing it could be one of them next.

Cynthia and the rest of his family were having a hard time grappling with the fact that the sheriff and the county administrators would sink that low. Welcome to his life for the past few years.

SIXTEEN

The game turned ugly more quickly than Matt expected, and the first blow was struck in the form of a letter published in the local paper. Written by a secretary from the city's police department, it appeared on the editor's page. Blaming Matt for 'biting the hand that feeds him,' she stated that he should 'be ashamed of himself.'

Matt knew it was the handiwork of the sheriff and his buddies. It seemed they had no problem telling straight-out lies. Since the public demotion hadn't worked as planned, thanks to that reporter from Farmington, Catlin was now taking harder tactics. Matt was tired of all the crap being spread about him, and he decided to take his case to the public by sending his own letter to the editor of the same paper.

Describing his last day at the sheriff's office, he wrote about nearly being killed while trying to stop the fleeing fugitives. "I put my life on the line in order to do my job and protect the public. I did so even though it was my last day at work. In return, I have been treated like discarded garbage."

He stated that neither Sheriff Catlin nor Captain Sanchez had visited or called him while he was in the hospital recovering from his wounds, nor since he had returned home. He ended the letter by stating, "If this is the way Sanchez treats his own people, how is he going to treat you, the public, if he is elected sheriff?"

Matt was aware his letter would really aggravate them, but he wanted the public to know what the truth was. A picture of Matt on crutches was featured on the paper's front page and was titled "Injured Cop Blasts Department for Lack of Support." The editor made sure Sanchez and the sheriff were given copies of his letter prior to the story being run, yet the same courtesy had not been extended to him.

Sheriff Catlin immediately issued a statement. "I have been to Matt's house three times since he returned home and I have called at least twice. I don't know what he's talking about."

To Matt, the whole scenario was becoming more and more surreal. Of course Catlin lied about it. The truth would rock his credibility, so he was brazenly making up stories as he went along.

The day following Matt's letter, another letter was written to the paper, this time from a detective at the city's police department. He wrote that Matt was using his injuries to make a political statement, and that he was 'disgusting.' Matt had been expecting rebuttals from the sheriff's office, but he was puzzled by the two letters from the local police department. He didn't know the people who wrote the letters, so all he could do was speculate as to why they did.

Two days later, a letter written by former Sergeant Tom Hill, who was now officially running against Sanchez for sheriff, praised Matt highly for the kind of cop he was. He wrote of how Matt had been the only cop out there who had actually tried to physically stop the fugitives by using his car as a blockade and that he did so all alone.

Matt's heart filled with gratitude at Tom's public words. That meant a lot to him, especially now when he felt he was once more standing alone against an enemy … this time his own department. A few law enforcement officers from different agencies also wrote letters in support of Matt, yet it seemed none of the citizens really cared. A majority of the locals blindly sided with the powerful sheriff and Juan Sanchez.

* * *

The town was abuzz about the feud that had sprung up between Matt and the sheriff's office. Sheriff Catlin and Sanchez had reportedly been surprised when Matt used the newspaper to fight back. They thought he would approach them personally, but they had not considered him going public. It had upset them to read letters from cops with other agencies who wrote in favor of Matt, praising his bravery against the heavily-armed fugitives.

Since everyone in the sheriff's office now supported Catlin, the momentum against Matt rose up like a muddy riptide coming in from the dregs of the sea, attempting to drown out the truth. It was Kangaroo justice at its best.

It seemed Sanchez was worried that all the negative publicity would hurt his campaign, so he and Catlin decided to embellish the rumors about Matt. They spread more false dirt about his character and loyalty, and the townspeople began to side more with the sheriff.

Matt was being branded the traitor who had quit the sheriff's office to go over to the Highway Patrol and was now forcing his old department to feed his family and pay his bills. After all, hadn't it been *his* choice to resign, so why should the sheriff's office have to support him? Once those rumors had circulated, the sheriff let the public know that, in spite of Matt's decision to quit, he was sympathetic and would be keeping Matt on the payroll for as long as needed.

Of course, he failed to say the law required him to keep Matt on, and that as long as he was at home, he was to be paid by Workman's Compensation and the last of his sick time hours. If he was forced to return before he was ready to go to the Academy, he would go back on the sheriff's payroll.

Matt was prepared for the type of venom being spread about him, but he was disappointed when so many people believed it. The sheriff and Sanchez wanted him gone, but couldn't fire him because he was now covered under the Disabilities Act. Therefore they had set out to attack him in any way they could, hoping to force him to quit again, this time under a cloud of suspicion.

Lately, he and Cynthia had begun feeling a chill from the community whenever they went out in public. He had not completely recovered from the second surgery to his knee yet, and his leg was swathed in bandages under his pants. Still in a lot of pain, his morale was spiraling downward again.

When yet another negative article appeared in the paper, Cynthia talked him into going to the local Wal-Mart, thinking he needed to get out of the house. It turned out to be a bad idea.

While she went looking for a cart near the front of the store, he walked over to a bench and sat down to wait for her. His leg was hurting, and he was hesitant to put too much weight on it yet. Unexpectedly, an older man wearing a hat that said "Sanchez for sheriff" disdainfully marched up to him and started shaking his finger close to Matt's face. The man spoke loudly, causing heads to turn. "Shame on you! Shame on you, Nelson! You're disgusting!"

Matt felt his hand tighten into a fist, and it took a lot of willpower not to bust the guy in the mouth. He was struggling to his feet when Cynthia rushed up to step between him and the man spewing out malice. She got right in the man's red, blustery face and said, "You have NO IDEA what the truth is here, mister! Why don't you check your facts before you go accusing someone who risked his life for people like you!"

The man was taken aback. "This ain't about you, lady."

Matt grabbed the man's arm in an iron grip. "Watch what you say to my wife."

Cynthia turned to look at Matt and pulled at his arm. "Come on, Honey. Let's get out of here. He isn't worth our time."

People in the store were staring at them, but as she and Matt walked out, they all turned away. No more visits to Wal-mart in this town.

The incident didn't help his mood any. He had never hesitated to put his life on the line to protect citizens like the man in Wal-Mart. It had shaken him to see the hate in that guy's eyes, then to witness other customers turn their backs on him as he exited the store. A majority of their community didn't seem to care when scapegoats were made of the innocent.

It suddenly seemed that he was fighting one battle after another and, later that day, he went through a whole gamut of strong, surging feelings that ranged from frustration to anger to despondency. Cynthia was so agitated, she wanted to go on television and tell the world about this part of the Four Corners area. If not for their faith, it would have been harder getting through the darkness created by an ignorant community which had passed judgment on them without knowing the whole truth.

* * * *

Two days after the Wal-Mart incident, Matt woke up ready to take on the sheriff's office and whoever else stood in his way. He quietly moved away from Cynthia, trying to get out of bed without waking her. Just as he swung his legs over the edge of the bed, she reached out to touch his hand.

Matt stopped and spoke softly, "You awake, Honey?"

She mumbled, "Uh-huh."

"I've made a decision. I'll be back shortly."

Her eyes looked sleepy. "What? Where are you going?"

He smiled. "You rest. I'll tell you when I get back." He kissed her and stood up, reaching for his jeans hanging over a chair. He grabbed the crutches as he walked out the door and was soon headed toward town.

His destination was the hardware store where he purchased a large poster board, a black marker and some tape. He made up a sign saying "Hill for sheriff" and placed it in the back window of his personal Jeep Cherokee. Once he had it secure, he stood back to look at his handiwork and grinned. "Let's see how they like that."

The sign lasted Monday and Tuesday, but when he and Cynthia walked out to their car on Wednesday morning, they discovered a big black "X" painted across the back window of their Jeep, blocking out their sign. It had been done with black shoe polish.

Cynthia gasped. "I can't believe they actually did that!"

Matt felt anger rising from his stomach. "You know what? No one has the right to tell me how to vote."

Cynthia was upset. "This is behavior you might expect from high school students!"

"It's not over." He proceeded to clean the shoe polish off his rear window so the sign could be seen again.

That evening, Cynthia opened the local paper and read a letter addressed to law enforcement agencies in the Four Corners area. It was from a police officer in West Virginia.

She glanced over at Matt who was watching a car race on cable and said, "Matt, I want to read you this letter on the editorial page."

Matt gave her a questioning look. "Good or bad?"

"Just listen. A police officer from Virginia wrote this after reading about the manhunt. He says he knows how law enforcement agencies can *disagree* on many things, but that when one of them is in danger, everyone comes running to help."

Matt nodded. "Okay."

"He says he commends the citizens of Cortez for their support of the officers involved in the search and the officers who were victims. He believes that when a community shows support for their police officers, it helps those officers who were hurt more than anyone could possibly know."

Matt listened as Cynthia read the letter, then said, "Well, he can't be talking about the community here. At least not the majority of it."

Cynthia put the paper down and sighed. "Since Catlin and Sanchez knew why you resigned, they should have put aside any disagreements they may have had about you. You nearly got killed! Besides, if dispatch had gotten you the right information, you wouldn't have taken on *three* dangerous men armed with assault rifles! Maybe they think you're going to sue them."

Matt nodded, thinking back to the shooting and the events leading up to it. He had been shot after eight law enforcement officers were stopped in their tracks, yet no one bothered to relay information over the radio that there were *three* fugitives, not just one, and that they were all armed with assault weapons.

Staring out the window, he noted, "I've tried to tell people the truth. The community seemed pretty compassionate at first … until that demotion appeared in the paper. I guess they think that where there's smoke, there's fire."

Her eyes blazed. "The sheriff is to blame for that! The public believes him, not you. I almost lost you, and not one deputy or their wives came around to console me or help in any way. Worse, they weren't there for *you*. You've always known what to do when it came to the bad guys, but you never thought the bad guys would turn out to be the people you worked with."

Matt nodded, "I didn't like it when Catlin used trickery to get me to quit. But I knew in the long run, I was going on to better things. What really rubs me the wrong way is how I was treated after being shot."

She shook her head. "Public figures don't think they have to answer to anyone today. Even Catholic priests can turn out to be child molesters who get out of jail time because the Catholic Church is so powerful."

Matt grimaced as he stretched his leg out. "Well, I wouldn't trade places with the lot of them."

Cynthia was a slim woman, only five-feet-four inches tall, but she was ready to take on Catlin and Sanchez personally. Her green eyes narrowed in determination. "We're going to prove they're liars, Matt. God willing, you are going to make the next Academy, and even if Sanchez wins the election, Catlin will have to answer for all his lies."

Matt felt a grin crawling along the edges of his mouth. "This is a vision you're getting, I hope?"

She laid the paper down, rose from the table and walked over to join him on the couch. Snuggling against him, she said, "Who cares what any of them say? One good thing has come from all this. We've sure found out who our real friends are."

SEVENTEEN

Five months after the shooting
....

It was the first week of October, just as the election was heating up, when Matt received a call from Undersheriff Warner.

Without one inquiry about Matt's health, he came right to the point. "Your sick leave is up at the end of October. If you're not back to work by then, you won't get paid."

Then he hung up.

Matt looked at the phone and slowly hung it up. He immediately called his doctor and received permission to return to work as long as he refrained from vigorous physical activity. He sent the release to Warner and received a note back, stating, "Do not return to work until after the election."

He and Cynthia read the note together, and Matt raised his eyebrows. "Guess I'm not wanted until the victory party is over."

Cynthia was more upset than he was. "I don't want you to go back there."

"It's not what I would choose. But we've got bills to pay."

She put her arms around him and burrowed her face against his chest. "I feel like we're living a nightmare. All because three guys decided to steal a truck on your last day at the sheriff's office. If they'd waited one more day, none of this would be happening."

He hugged her, but didn't know what to say. Fate had allowed him to be out there at that precise time, but now it was up to him to do everything he could to get back on track and into the Academy.

* * *

Juan Sanchez won the election just as Matt predicted and a huge celebration party was thrown the next day. Of course, he wasn't invited.

When he returned to work on the day after the election, he found the parking lot totally empty and the doors locked. He no longer had his gun or vest because they had been taken from him at the scene of the shooting.

They had also taken his badge after he had returned home from the hospital. A deputy had come out to his house and said, "They want your badge, Matt. I assume it's because you're on sick leave and all."

So he was now without identification and driving his own personal car on his first day back. Using his old key, he entered the building to find no one there. It must have been quite a party the night before. As he returned to his old office, he began settling in, not sure what the day would bring. However, he suspected it would not be one worth remembering.

When Sheriff Catlin eventually showed up, he walked by Matt's office and looked in. "I'll be damned. You made it."

"Was there a question?"

The sheriff ignored him and said, "Guess the election didn't turn out like you wanted."

Matt shrugged his shoulders. "I exercised my right to vote, and that's what counts."

Sheriff Catlin's eyes shifted, and his mouth slowly formed a smug-looking smile as he walked on by.

Twenty minutes later, Matt's phone buzzed. It was the sheriff. "I want to see you in my office."

Matt pushed himself up, feeling stiff and slightly painful, and walked down the hall to Catlin's office. At least the crutches were gone, but he hated it when the limp got more pronounced after sitting for a time.

In Catlin's office, Matt sat down on a high-backed chair facing the aggravated man he still had to report to. Neither said a word at first, then the sheriff broke the silence. "I don't get it."

"You don't get what?"

Long pause. "I don't get it."

"I don't understand."

Another long pause. "I can't believe you're actually here."

"Why wouldn't I be here? I got a note telling me to come in today or not get paid."

"I wrote that note."

Matt looked at his watch. "This is the day I was told to come in and I'm here to work." He knew he was being flippant, but at that point he really didn't care.

Catlin's face flushed, and anger flashed in his eyes. "You can't be trusted!"

Matt frowned. "What makes you think that?"

"I will *never* get ambushed again!"

Matt was confused for a moment; then he remembered the reporter from Farmington. "Oh. You mean the reporter. He already had it figured out. He asked, and I told him the truth."

"Yeah, you certainly did that."

Matt stared at Catlin. "Why *did* you use the paper to demote me … as though I had done something wrong?"

"There's only one guy callin' the shots around here, Nelson. And it's not you."

It wasn't exactly an answer to his question, but he knew it was the best he was going to get.

That conversation set the pace for the rest of the day. As he started to walk outside at five o'clock, he felt tired, achy and frustrated. He had come within an inch of quitting an hour ago, but he kept himself in check.

Before he could get out the door, Sheriff Catlin stopped him and thrust a small box at him. "Here. This is yours. They were handed out at the awards' ceremony you didn't attend."

Matt took the box and brushed past Catlin to go out the door and down the hall. Once outside, he walked quickly to his car and scooted onto the driver's seat, shutting the door as he got in. Only then did he open the box. Inside was a Medal of Valor. He knew Juan Sanchez had also received one, along with several others in the office.

He was also aware that Juan Sanchez got his medal for ducking down in his car when he got shot at by the fleeing fugitives. *Gee, maybe I should have thought of that.*

When he entered the apartment that evening, he leaned against the door jamb and looked at Cynthia. "Getting shot didn't hurt as much as this hurts."

She went to him and hugged him tightly. "I'm so sorry, Honey."

He handed her the box with the medal in it. "Here. This just doesn't mean a lot to me right now."

She looked inside, then up at him. "I don't understand."

He told her how the sheriff had treated him from the moment he had arrived at the office and how he had given the box to him as he was leaving for the day.

Her eyes registered her anger. "They've cheapened what the Medal of Valor stands for! Please don't go back there!"

"Cynthia, I don't exactly have a choice right now. But you know what? I'm going to make it just fine. Those people aren't worth losing any sleep over."

He felt he was physically ready to try out for the Academy, but he had to wait for an official invitation. In the meantime, they had to eat.

* * *

On Matt's second day back, everyone had returned to work. He instantly got the cold shoulder from everyone, including the deputies who had served with him on the SWAT team. Whether in the halls or the main lobby of the sheriff's office, it was the same. They would pass by without the slightest acknowledgment of his presence. It was a difficult day, but he kept his cool and tried to rise above it.

That afternoon, he walked by one of the secretaries as she was talking to two deputies. As soon as she noticed him, she stopped talking until he had passed them. Suddenly laughter broke out, followed by a couple of loud-mouthed hoots and one deputy exclaimed, "The best man won!"

Matt hesitated before entering his office, then turned to look straight at them. "In case everyone's forgotten, we all have the right to vote for whomever we choose. In my opinion, the best man did *not* win."

He then walked back into his small office and shut the door behind him. Sitting down at his desk, he put his feet up and took a deep, satisfying breath. If he had been a smoker, a big fat cigar would have been appropriate at that moment. Why hadn't he seen how narrow-minded the whole office was before now? Guess he'd been doing his job while everyone else was making judgment calls and following the sheriff's rear end around.

I may be handicapped right now, but I wouldn't change places with one person in this abyss they call a law enforcement department.

EIGHTEEN

On November 10th, Matt's third day back, sheriff-elect Sanchez, Detective Groggin, the deputy who had taken over Matt's position when he quit, and Undersheriff Warner were furtively talking in a cluster when he entered the main door that led into the lobby. Once again they all immediately quit talking when they saw him. Matt nodded in their direction but continued to walk toward his office.

Within minutes, Undersheriff Warner was standing in his doorway. "Matt, I want to see you in Groggin's office right now."

Matt's chest tightened. *What now?*

He walked down the hall and entered Groggin's new office to find Warner standing while Groggin was ensconced behind his desk. Without a word of greeting, Warner informed him he was going to be loaned out to the City Police Department to help with the task force on 'remaining fugitive issues'.

The Undersheriff looked pleased as he slowly smiled. "Since you'll be starting tomorrow, you won't need to report back here anymore. In fact, why don't you go on home now?"

Matt was taken by surprise. He nodded. "Okay. I can do that."

He was thinking this was the best news he had received since he walked through the door three days ago. He liked the guys over at the City Police Department and had always appreciated the kindness and concern they had shown him since the shooting. *With the exception of those who had written those poison letters to the paper.*

Matt returned to his office and quickly packed up his personal things, which weren't much. He couldn't get out of there fast enough. Holding everything in his arms, he exited the sheriff's office just as he had entered it three days ago … with his head held high. As the door closed behind him, he heard laughter coming out through the window. All he felt was total relief as he walked to his Jeep. Now he could concentrate on getting into the Academy!

* * *

Cynthia had heard his car pull into the driveway and quickly opened the door to greet him, but he could see the worry in her eyes. He'd only been gone an hour since he left for work that morning. "Matt! Is everything okay?"

He grinned widely and said, "Everything's great, Honey."

"Why? Did you quit, I hope?"

"Nah. They decided they don't want the pleasure of my company anymore, so I've been banished over to the City Police Department. I start tomorrow."

She looked at him in surprise. "Permanently?"

"I'm sure they'd like that, but I'm going to the Academy before that happens."

* * *

Matt began spending every spare moment he could building up his strength. He forced his body to move beyond what most people could ever cope with and it was working. Each day he could move a little faster and last a little longer.

It was Friday, and he had been working for three weeks at the city police department when he received the news he had been praying for. The Highway Patrol Office called his home to say he had been accepted for the next Academy!

He and Cynthia were jubilant! They celebrated that weekend, driving over to Durango to have dinner at the Stratter Hotel. Afterwards, they went to a local nightclub and danced together for the first time since the shooting. Deciding to splurge, they later returned to the Stratter Hotel and rented a suite overlooking the downtown streets. Cuddling together in a big, four poster bed covered with down comforters, it seemed all the months of rehabilitation and pain and frustration were behind him now. He had made it!

* * *

Monday morning, he walked into the sheriff's office and to everyone's astonishment, asked to speak to Undersheriff Warner. When he entered

Warner's office, he stood in front of his desk and waited until the Undersheriff looked up at him.

Warner gave him a questioning look. "Yeah, Matt? What is it you want?" He appeared nervous.

Matt was holding his picture identification in his right hand. It was the only I.D. he had in his possession, since neither his gun nor badge had ever been returned to him.

Tossing the I.D. on Warner's desk, Matt said, "I know this isn't going to break anyone's heart, but I quit."

Warner's lip curled up into a half smile that didn't reach his eyes. "Yeah?"

"Don't take it too hard."

The Undersheriff's voice sounded lame to Matt's ears. "Now, Matt. No need to be sarcastic. I'm sorry things haven't gone better for you, but …"

Matt interrupted him. "You know what disappointed me the most? Having my own guys turn their backs on me. But hey, that's over now. It's time to move on."

Warner looked uncomfortable. "So what are you gonna' do now?"

Matt met his eyes, feeling damned good. "Me? I'm going to the Colorado Highway Patrol."

NINETEEN

....

It was January 1999 when Matt arrived at the Academy in Golden, Colorado. He was about to embark on another part of his journey, one that would challenge him almost as much as overcoming his wounds.

He was given a sparse-looking cot alongside other cots in a large dorm-like room. His first big task was to make his bed over six times. The drill master demanded it be made according to his strict instructions, or he would destroy the whole bed and make you do it again until it was perfect. *That was a lot of fun.*

The yelling began immediately, just like in boot camp. He decided if he could make it through that day, he could go the distance. Pushups had always been considered basic, and he had always been good at them. The arm pull-ups proved to be the most punishing because of his injured left arm, but he found a way to compensate for it by bearing most of his weight on his right arm. The Drill Master didn't object because he was easily keeping up with the others.

He called Cynthia at the end of that first day, exhausted but exhilarated. "I made it, Baby. It's going to be okay."

Cynthia didn't tell him, but she had been in agony all day. She tried to keep the worry out of her voice and asked, "How is your arm?"

"It hurts, but it's not unbearable. They're letting me use my right arm with the pull-ups, and that's working out well. As long as I get the job done, they don't care."

Hearing his words sent a rush of relief through her. "That's good, Honey. That's really good. So, how do you like making your own bed again?"

He laughed. "I only had to make it over six times this morning."

"Six! What happened?" She started laughing.

"What can I say? I've been a spoiled man."

"Yeah? Well, since you're becoming such an expert now, you can start making the bed here."

"I'd rather 'unmake' the bed … as long as you help me."

When they hung up, Cynthia was smiling. For the first time since Matt had driven off to attend the academy, she felt peaceful. He sounded so assured and happy, just like the days before the shooting. He was strong, tough and determined. He had pushed himself to the breaking point to get to the academy, but now that he had made it, he wasn't going to take chances with his arm or leg. She knew in her heart that he would go all the way.

* * *

Matt understood that the greatest challenge for him would be the running. He wasn't confident of how his injured knee would hold up, so when he was told they wouldn't be required to run the whole three miles all at once, he was greatly relieved. The Drill Master started everyone out at one mile and gradually built up their distance. He didn't have any trouble running that mile.

Over the next few weeks, he continued to improve physically and found himself getting more fit each day. During the Arrest/Control exercises, he had to modify things once more to compensate for his damaged left arm. As far as his Drill Master was concerned, that wasn't a problem, and he even informed Matt of how well he was doing. Matt felt gratified because he didn't want to throw up any red flags that would make them think they had to take it easy on him. He kept his aches and pains to himself, thankful each day for the chance to be there.

Since January that year was proving to be an exceptionally stormy month, dumping lots of snow and ice all across Colorado, the cadets had added challenges, but that was the trade-off for living in the mountains.

It was dark when he finally headed his Jeep toward the Western Slope for his first weekend home with Cynthia. Snow was already falling as his car began climbing up the Uncompahgre River Canyon toward the summit of Red Mountain Pass. The Pass was always a risk in the winter and he had to go over the top of it to get home.

The snow flakes were taking on a strobe-like look as they came down in front of his headlights. He had put the defroster on in order to keep the windows from icing up and checked his seat belt. The further he went, the thicker the snow became, and visibility was soon almost down to zero.

He saw no other cars ahead or behind him and knew there were stretches along the pass where there were no guard rails. Since his cell phone wouldn't work here, a feeling of isolation engulfed him as he drove toward the peak of the suddenly perilous mountain. The pass sat at 11,000 feet, and he could no longer see where the edge of the road was.

As his Jeep slowly plowed through the deepening snow, he saw a faint light shining through the pitch darkness of the night. The welcome sight of a large snowplow bore down on him and pulled up beside his car.

Matt recognized the driver and rolled down his window, squinting through the blowing snow. "Hey, Dave! Am I glad to see you tonight."

The driver peered into the car and broke into a big smile. "Matt Nelson! What are you doin' up here, son?"

"I'm heading home to my wife. What's it like up ahead?"

"It's gettin' worse. But you should be able to make Silverton before they close the road."

"I take it you won't be coming back this way."

"Not tonight. You're almost to that big slide area, so stay right where I just plowed and you should be okay. It looks like we'll get at least two feet tonight."

"Are they going to shoot down some avalanches?" It was the practice to use explosives to knock down heavy snow buildup above the passes.

Dave shook his head. "Don't know yet. When's that Academy done with?"

"It's just started, so it'll be awhile."

Dave stared at him, the big truck rumbling and shaking. "For what it's worth, I think it was a damned shame how the sheriff's office treated you."

He rolled up his window and continued on down the Pass, disappearing from view within seconds. Matt rolled up his window and turned the heater on high. He was surprised. Evidently there were others in the area who saw through the crap and recognized the truth of what had happened to him.

Smiling, he put the Jeep in low four-wheel drive and it lurched forward toward Silverton. This storm was not going to stop him from going down into Delores. He had a warm bed and Cynthia waiting for him below.

* * *

By February, he had become a real pro at crossing over the Red Mountain Pass in the snow. It was the last weekend of the month and he was almost home. The weather had improved this month, for which he was appreciative. Fog-chilled air filtered through the pines as he pulled up in front of their fairly isolated house in a dead-end canyon on the outskirts of Delores. The fog drifted toward their house like fingers of clouds, and snow lay in patches here and there.

When he let himself into the darkened house, he saw the bedroom light go on and suddenly Cynthia was rushing toward him. He grinned and held out his arms, enclosing her tightly within them.

She looked up at him, her face drawn. "I'm so glad you're home!"

He caught the sense of anxiety in her voice. "So am I. Is something wrong?"

She pointed to their large picture window, now tightly draped. "Ranger started barking at the window last night and when I looked, I saw a man looking in at me. A tall man dressed in *camouflage*! He must have been standing on our planter box. He just walked off into the trees, like he didn't have a care in the world. It was Jay Vista, Matt."

Vista was one of the fugitives who had escaped capture. "Slow down, Honey. It doesn't make sense that one of those guys would come here when the whole country's looking for them."

"Not 'them,' Matt. *Him.* It was Vista. The man is crazy, and he hates cops. His cousin lives right down the road, remember? Maybe that's where he's been hiding out, and he knows this is our house."

"Did you call the police?"

"I called Julie. Guy was out on patrol, and she said I should call the sheriff's office. But I couldn't call them for obvious reasons, so Ranger and I just kept alert the rest of the night. The next morning I found footprints near the planter and out under the trees."

Now he was more than a little bothered. "So Guy never stopped by last night?"

"He called first thing this morning. I guess he thinks it's probably a window peeker. Matt, who would come to our house dressed in camouflage and stare in our front window? The man was tall and thin, just like Vista. I couldn't see his face because he wore something dark over it … like a ski mask or something." Her voice grew quiet. "Like the fugitives wore."

Matt shook his head. "It doesn't make sense. Did Guy say he was going to check it out further?"

"Yeah, but he's been getting panic calls from everybody in the county. What if it was a message to *you*? Does Vista want you to know he's alive and well?"

"Calm down, Honey. First thing in the morning, I'll call Guy's office and try to find out what he thinks about it. Okay?"

She nodded and reached up to touch his face, noticing how tired he looked. "Okay. I'm sorry, Honey. You've been gone all week and I've been missing you so much. Let's just forget everything and go to bed."

He smiled and pulled her into his arms. "You know, I *am* tired. It's been a hard week. I bet I fall asleep the moment my head hits the pillow."

She looked up at him, her eyes questioning. "Oh yeah?"

He laughed softly. "No. No way."

* * *

The next day, Matt called Guy at the Highway Patrol office in Durango. Guy agreed it had seemed strange that someone would go to all the trouble of dressing in camouflage and look in the window at Cynthia.

"Sounds like this guy made it a point to be seen."

That didn't sit well with Matt. "She said he had something over his face. Like a ski mask. What the hell was that all about? Was he trying to scare her because he knows I'm at the Academy?"

"Look, I know this is a sore subject, but you're not real popular down at the sheriff's office. Would one of your former buddies try something like this?"

"Nah. They wouldn't go after her."

"Okay. Then let's assume it was Vista or one of his militia friends. Or his cousin. Why be so obvious?"

"Who knows what those guys think? I'm going to ask if she'll go to her mother's for awhile, but I doubt that she will. Could you keep an eye on her and the house during the week?"

"You bet. Hey, don't worry too much, Matt. I hear she's a dead shot with that nine millimeter you bought her. And she's got her big dog. She'll be okay."

"Yeah, well, I'll still feel better if you do some drive-bys."

"You can count on it, Matt."

The weekend flew, and it was soon time to return to Golden. He didn't feel easy leaving Cynthia all alone again. "Honey, until we know more about whoever was in the yard, why don't you stay with your mother? Just until the Academy is over?"

Her eyes flared. "No. This is our home, and I'm not going to let anyone scare me away."

He knew he wasn't going to change her mind. "Okay, but I don't want you taking any chances. If something looks wrong, call Guy or anyone at the office. Better to be safe than …"

She reached out and put her arms around him, laying her head against his chest. "I promise I won't do anything stupid. If I get worried, I'll go stay with Mom. Deal?"

He felt slightly better. "Deal."

As his Jeep began to ascend the steep pass back toward Silverton, Matt thought about the man in their yard. The fact that the guy took the trouble to dress like he did was disturbing. Maybe one of the militia guys living in the area wanted to send a message to him, just as Cynthia had suggested. But it hadn't been personal between him and those guys. He was doing his job and they had nearly killed him. If anyone wanted to make it personal, it should be him.

Maybe it *was* Vista's cousin who lived nearby. Damn. Cynthia's hunches had proven to be right on the button more often than not. *Especially on his last day at work.* He was glad he had talked with Guy, and that the Officer would be watching over her and the house.

TWENTY

As the weeks went by, Cynthia had no further sightings of the camouflaged-clad man near her home and she began to put the whole incident out of her mind. She knew what she had seen, but maybe it wasn't as ominous as she had first thought. Maybe it had been the cousin and he was satisfied with having scared her.

One Saturday, she made a luncheon date with Josie, a girlfriend from Silverton, and was surprised when her friend asked, "After all you and Matt have been through, don't you worry about him staying in the police field?"

Cynthia frowned. "That's up to Matt. I married a cop, and we talked about his career before we got married."

Josie nodded. "Well, I admire both of you very much. I don't think I could do what you've done."

"I admit this whole thing has been difficult, but thank God Matt not only survived, but also made the Academy. It was a close call."

Josie nodded. "It was, and you fought the battle right there at his side."

"Thanks, but I'll be so glad when this Academy is over. Matt is still healing, and he's been pushing himself so hard." She shrugged her shoulders. "I just don't want him to overdo it."

Josie reached across the table and patted Cynthia's hand. "Knowing Matt, he'll be careful. He's not going to take any chances that would cost him his future as a cop."

Cynthia loosened up. "I know that, so why do I worry? Right now, I feel like having a glass of red wine while you tell me all the latest gossip."

Josie laughed. "How long do we have?"

When she and Josie parted, Cynthia knew how happy she would be to have Matt home again. She just wanted their lives to be normal again; at least as normal as they would ever be.

TWENTY-ONE

At the academy, Matt was finding out he could not only keep up with men in their twenties, but also was actually surpassing them despite his injuries. The classroom work came easy for him because he had already been in law enforcement for nine years. In that regard, he was pretty self-confident.

He found it hard to believe that spring was just around the corner and that meant the rigors of the Academy were almost over. A couple of weeks prior to graduation, one of his instructors took him aside and said, "When you first showed up, I really didn't think you'd make it, Matt. We all had our doubts. Glad to say you proved us wrong."

Matt understood their concern and nodded. "I'm just happy I had the chance to try. Thank you, Sir."

* * *

One year after the shooting

In June of 1999, Matt became a Colorado State Trooper.. His long and painful journey to make it through rehabilitation and then the Academy was over.

It was a big day for him. His whole family traveled to Golden to see him graduate: his son, his mother and father, his brother and in-laws. Of course, Cynthia was right at his side.

As they sat near the stage that evening, Matt whispered to Cynthia, "I guess some awards are being handed out before we get our certificates."

Cynthia eyes showed her pride. "Okay. So, are you up for an award?"

He chuckled. "Every cadet here is eligible, so don't get your hopes up."

When the first award was given that evening, he was surprised to hear his name being called. He smiled at Cynthia and squeezed her hand, then stood up amidst the applause and went onstage to shake hands with his supervisors. He had barely returned to his seat when his name was called again. He saw how his family was beaming with pride as he returned to the stage and, though he felt slightly self-conscious, he also felt pretty damned good. He had succeeded beyond his wildest dreams.

The Chief of the Colorado Highway Patrol shook his hand and told the audience about his long battle to overcome almost impossible odds. He went on to say, "If one measures the size of a man's accomplishments by the obstacles he overcomes to reach his goals … then Matt Nelson has a lot to be proud of."

When he asked Matt to say something, Matt found himself hesitating. Public speaking had never been one of his stronger points; however, he needed to give it his best shot.

Thanking his supervisors, he spoke into the mike, "Well … I have to say this has been the climax to a life-altering year. My whole world was turned around in one instant last May. With the help of my wife, Cynthia, and family and friends … I made it. Tonight has made up for it all. I'm looking forward to a long career with the Highway Patrol."

The audience applauded loudly, but Matt was centered on his wife and family. That they were there to witness his accomplishments in light of his handicaps was the highlight of the evening.

The dark days following the shooting, when everyone at the sheriff's office had turned their backs on him instead of pouring out the support he needed so much, had been rough. He had done his best against trained 'survivalists' who were using armored bullets that easily tore his Jeep apart. His knee and elbow had been shattered; transformed into jello.

Mentally, it had left a scar that would never completely go away, but it had also made him stronger and wiser. He and Cynthia had faced all the fabrications the sheriff had spread about him, held their heads high and gone forward. They believed in themselves and God, and they had persevered.

TWENTY-TWO

Since Matt had graduated at the top of his class, he was given his choice of nineteen posts available within Colorado. He chose Silverton, the small mountain village north of Durango that sat encircled by wild country and towering mountains. To get there from Durango, you had to take the winding, narrow Million Dollar Highway with its hairpin curves, sheer drop-offs and 10,000 foot passes.

It was a one-man station, and the State Patrol was more than pleased to employ an experienced officer there. While summers in the San Juan Mountains often boast 70-degree weather, Matt knew personally how rough the winters could be, with snowfall averaging two-hundred inches a year.

The Search and Rescue team there in Silverton had a motto: *If you need our help, you really need help!*

Yet there was no place he knew that was more beautiful. He would be content to spend the rest of his life there.

Once he started his post, he and Cynthia decided to put their Delores house on the market and move up to Silverton. It was time to cut all ties with Cortez and the canyonlands and the painful memories. Cynthia's dream was to open a small coffee shop on Main Street in Silverton, which also happened to be the only paved street through town.

Silverton boasts a wonderful old courthouse built in 1907, beautifully restored Victorian hotels decorated in romantic nostalgic pieces from the mining days, quaint bed and breakfast inns and, sitting at 10,500 feet, the Molas Lake Park. Close to the tiny city is the Hundred-Year-Old Gold Mine, where you can take a tour deep into the heart of the 13,728 foot Galena Mountain.

They found the perfect empty commercial building on Main Street with a two-bedroom apartment over it. The lower space would soon become her coffee shop, and they decided to live in the overhead apartment until their Delores house sold.

As Cynthia became busier and busier with her opening plans for the coffee shop, Matt found himself content and happy with his new job. Because his life had been so traumatic and complicated for the last year, it was pure magic to be living and working in the San Juans.

Unlike past experiences with the sheriff's office, he now received daily support from the Highway Patrol. Even though he was pretty much on his own up here in the mountains, with the nearest Highway Patrol Officer an hour away, he found himself liking the solitude of his post.

It had become a running joke within the circle of his fellow Patrol Officers that he was to warn them if he decided to retire. They said they all planned on being somewhere else when that day arrived —- especially if there was a cake!

Even though they said it in jest, Matt now found himself being more cautious when he was out there by himself. He had developed what is called a survivor's mindset and would often play out certain scenarios in his mind, then decide how he would survive them.

The fact that he had not only lived through the shooting, but also had come as far as he had, made him believe that there *was* a guardian angel watching over him. God had other plans for him than to die on that church driveway last year and he was going to take full advantage of his second chance at life.

Matt's silver and blue patrol car was a familiar sight on the long, winding highway leading to the sky. It made him feel good whenever he aided travelers, whether they had had a narrow escape on the highway or just needed help changing a flat tire. He especially liked pulling night patrol. It was usually quiet then, with few people on the roads.

One night he came around a curve up near Molas Lake and the high beam of a car parked on the side of the road lit up his whole car. He quickly yanked the cruiser onto the right shoulder of the road and slammed on the brakes. Pulling out his gun, he saw someone get out of the car on the passenger side and start toward him. Matt yelled out, "Stay where you are! Don't move!"

A man's voice called out in fear, "God, don't shoot, Matt! It's me! John Beaver!"

Matt aimed his cruiser spotlight on the parked car and saw another figure in the driver's seat. The man standing outside the car *was* John Beaver! What the heck was he doing up here in the middle of the night? "Come on out here where I can see you better, John. Who's in the car?"

John began moving slowly toward Matt, his hands out where Matt could see them. "That's my son, Rob. He's learning how to drive. I thought it would be safer this time of night."

Matt relaxed and holstered his gun. Taking his flashlight, he exited his car and approached John, saying, "Never turn your bright lights on a car like that. It blinds the driver, and it made me wonder if it was on purpose."

John was immediately apologetic. "I'm sorry, Matt! Rob didn't mean to do that! He's just learning and accidentally hit the brights."

Matt nodded. "I understand, John, but maybe it's not a good idea to be teaching your boy to drive on these mountain curves in the middle of the night, okay?"

"Yeah, I see what you mean. Well, guess I'll do the drivin' back home. Thanks, Matt. We'll see you later."

John returned to his car and walked over to the driver's side. Matt saw him gesturing for his son to scoot over so he could get behind the wheel himself. Waving, he turned the car around and headed back down the mountain.

You'd think Silverton's Town Manager would know better.

Matt returned to his patrol car and turned off everything but his parking lights. Stretching his legs, he leaned back against the car and looked up at the immense sky over his head. The stars looked like bright, twinkling candles floating over the dark peaks of the mountains. *What a great view. I need to bring Cynthia up here over the weekend. She could use a break from the coffee shop.*

Nights like this were one of the upsides to being a cop in the mountains. The stars soothed him and made him feel close to things eternal. Dawn was always a special magic hour. Nocturnal creatures were bedding down and the daytime birds and animals were beginning to wake up. Everything was quiet now, even the mighty San Juans.

Of course, there was always a downside. That constituted dealing with speeding cars and drunk drivers who drive like they're hell-bent on killing themselves and whoever got in their way. Sometimes kids would come up the mountain thinking they were driving in the annual race up Pike's Peak. It was always painful when he had to deal with fatalities, especially if a young child was involved.

He was fortunate there wasn't much crime on this particular highway, and Matt's shifts were pretty routine. Each day brought a new look to the mountains and skies, bringing with it an increased gratitude that he had made it through this past year.

Up here, he could set his watch by the first shrill blast from the whistle of the Durango/Silverton train as its coal-burning engine chugged its way up the mountains to Silverton. He was often able to spend his lunch hour at the now-open coffee shop with Cynthia and, on days when he didn't have to work, he enjoyed pitching in behind the counter. Long-time friends would stop by to share some coffee with them and talk about the latest happenings in the area.

The good life was slowly emerging through the lingering clouds, and even when the pain flared up on certain days, he didn't care. He was right where he wanted to be.

TWENTY-THREE

Sixteen months after the shootings

....

On the last day of the 1999 Labor Day weekend, Matt was in Silverton observing tourists as they exited the train to make their last bid for some vacation fun before school started. Cars had been almost bumper to bumper up the mountain all weekend, and he'd had to arrest several people for reckless driving while intoxicated. He was tired.

At exactly five o'clock, he turned his cruiser north and drove to Main Street, arriving at Cynthia's and his little apartment above the coffee shop a few minutes later. Since he'd been on duty since Thursday, he had been given the next four days off.

God, he was ready for a little rest and relaxation! His bones ached and he felt a headache coming on. The sun had been relentless today and because of the thinner air this high up, he needed to protect his skin. Cynthia was always warning him to use sunscreen and he tried to remember, but sometimes he was just too busy.

Cynthia had dinner waiting for him when he walked in the front door. Taking off his hat and gun and putting them away, he kissed her and gratefully sat down at the table to relax.

She looked at him anxiously. "It look's like you're limping."

"I'm just tired. I'm glad this weekend is finally over."

She had all the windows open, and he noticed how the evenings already had a sharper edge to them. Soon the leaves on the Aspens would change into the golden and red colors he loved as they prepared for the coming cold. In the crisp, fall days of autumn, everything seemed more defined, more pure. Even his mind felt sharper.

After dinner he helped Cynthia clean up, then went outside to sit on the balcony overlooking the street and stores below. The mountains loomed up over the small city and Matt was once again struck with the beauty here.

Cynthia soon joined him, snuggling close against him for body warmth. Smiling, he placed his arm around her and asked, "How did things go for you today?"

She sighed. "Good, but I don't think I sat down all afternoon. Just as I was getting ready to put up the 'closed' sign, Hank came in and drank the last of the coffee. He asked if there were any new leads on Jay Vista or Alec Column. Have you heard anything?"

Hank Thomas was a local resident who had befriended them, but Matt didn't know if he appreciated him bringing all that stuff up again. "Honey, I think they're both dead somewhere in a hidden ravine down in the canyonlands."

She looked at him, a frown creasing her forehead. "What if they're not? What if it's true that they're being helped by friends and different militia groups? You know how those groups like to hold meetings and make plans to overtake the government. Hank said there's an active group between here and Ouray. Did you know that?"

He kept his voice light. "Sure, I've heard about that group. Look, if it's true they're helping the fugitives, let's hope someone rats on them so we can bring them in for trial. I'd like to see closure on this too. Why did they steal that water truck? And why the hell did they go berserk like they did?"

"They know you're alone out there, Matt."

He looked in her eyes. "I just don't think about it, Cynthia. I'm always careful, and I can't be worrying about what might happen."

She hesitated, then said, "I know, but I listen to my gut feelings more now."

He leaned back against the wall and put his hands behind his head. "So what are your gut feelings telling you now?"

"Nothing specific. It's probably just Hank's questions that got me thinking about everything again. One thing I do know is that you were saved for a purpose, and those guys better not screw with your guardian angel."

He chuckled and pulled her against him. "Or the angel sitting beside me."

* * *

Halloween 1999
....

Matt received a message from dispatch telling him to call a news reporter in Albuquerque. It wasn't the anniversary of the shootings, and he wasn't aware of anything new concerning the fugitives, so he was surprised at the call. When he was able to take time to phone the reporter, he was caught off guard.

The reporter asked, "Officer Nelson, what did you think about the news?"

Matt was confused. "What news?"

"They found a second body today. They think it's one of the fugitives because of the camouflage clothing and the rifle."

"Yeah? I hadn't heard, but that's good news."

The reporter ended up asking for an interview and when Matt agreed, he and his crew drove up from Albuquerque that evening. Sitting in Cynthia's and his small apartment, the reporter got right to the point. "How do you feel about this second body being found? We've heard it's Alec Column."

The nurse's cousin.

Matt thought for a moment, then nodded. "Well, I can't say I'm sorry he's dead. He and his buddies killed a good cop and wounded several others."

"How do you feel about the third suspect, Jay Vista? Do you think he's still out there?"

"That's anyone's guess. I know we'd all like to see some kind of closure to this whole thing. It would be good if they could arrest him and bring him to trial. But if they find his bones out there, that's okay too. Justice will have been served either way."

He hesitated, then added. "Still, it would be satisfying to know just what they were planning to do with that truck."

The reporter noted that Column's body had been found by Navajo deer hunters. The fugitive's skeleton was sitting propped up against a juniper tree near Cross Canyon, the bones protruding through his camouflage clothing and bullet-proof vest.

A bullet hole was found in his skull and suicide was suspected once again, even though the downward angle of the bullet seemed suspicious. Column was found just two miles from where the flatbed truck had been abandoned during the first week of the manhunt. Matt was thinking that maybe Stone had been shot first, then Column a short time later.

He found himself once again questioning the suicide findings, and wondering whether Vista had shot both men, attempting to make it look like suicides. Was he the most dangerous of the three men and had Vista been the one standing outside their Delores house in February? Matt knew Cynthia never once thought it was Column. She had said it was Vista. There were too many questions and not enough answers.

When the reporter and his crew left, Cynthia turned to Matt, her face white. "So they *both* died of head wounds and now it looks like they died at almost the same time. Do you think Vista killed them?"

"It wouldn't surprise me. There's rarely much loyalty between guys like that. Bottom line is that they're dead, and that means two less guys to think about. And remember, it wasn't personal between them and me. They were gonna' mow down anyone who got in their way. They were desperate to get out of the situation they had created and I was one of the cops in their way."

She nodded. "I know, but it scares me when I think that five-hundred cops couldn't stop those guys. And the two who are dead *weren't* killed by cops."

He took her hand. "Hey, we're all more prepared today if something like that happens again, honey. I know one thing … I won't try being a human blockade again." He grinned, hoping to get things back to a lighter note.

She didn't smile back. "You'd better not, or I'm going back to Texas."

He pulled her close. "No, you won't."

A small smile began in her lower lip. "Don't be too sure, mister."

"I'll arrest you before you get out of town."

"I'll make your life miserable and you'll let me go just to get some peace."

"That I'll never do."

"So bribe me and maybe I'll stay."

He leaned over and gave her a quick kiss. "How about we drive over to Laughlin and get away for a couple of days?"

Laughlin, Nevada was one of their favorite places to go because it brought back memories of their wedding and the great time everyone had. They tried to go there a couple of times a year because it wasn't that far, yet they liked the anonymity they had while there. They usually stayed at Harrah's in a room that overlooked the river.

It was fun to do a little gambling and enjoy the abundance of food for reasonable prices. They also liked to take in some shows and later walk along the river walk at midnight.

Her face lit up. "Really?" Putting her arms around him, she smiled and said, "It's time I got to have you all to myself for awhile. It's been a long year."

His arms went around her, pulling her closer. "A damn long year. I don't want to talk about the fugitives or my job or the coffee shop. We'll check out the shows and eat some good food, and we'll do a little gambling."

His grinned. "We'll also make sure the hotel has a hot tub. What do you think?"

She stretched up to kiss him. "I think I'm going to start packing right now, and *nothing* is going to interfere."

In the next hour, she had arranged for her friend, Anya, to manage the coffee shop while they were gone. Anya lived in an apartment above the building next to the coffee shop, and she had helped out when Cynthia was first putting the shop together.

They left Silverton early Tuesday morning with plans to stay through Thursday afternoon. The moment they headed down the mountain in the direction of Laughlin, they felt carefree, both laughing and teasing each other. They rented a room at one of the casinos on the river, and Matt made sure a hot tub in their room was one of amenities.

After spending a day of gambling, catching a show and having a late dinner, they returned to their room, tired but not sleepy. Matt tuned the television set to a digital music station and Cynthia ran the water for the hot tub, surrounding it with candles she had bought in a hotel shop. It was romantic and healing.

Here, he wasn't Matt Nelson, Highway Patrol Trooper, and she wasn't the proprietor of one of the most successful shops in Silverton. They were newlyweds again; just the two of them with the outside world far away.

Thursday morning arrived too soon. Staying in bed until ten, they procrastinated as long as they could. Checkout time was eleven o'clock, so they showered quickly and packed their bags, then ate a late breakfast in the casino's restaurant. After they put their bags in their Jeep, Cynthia turned to Matt and grinned. "Come on. Let's walk over to Danny Laughlin's Casino and try our luck before we go home."

He raised his eyebrow. "You feeling lucky, I hope?" They had not won anything yet.

She shrugged her shoulders and gave him a sly grin. "Maybe. Are you?"

He locked the doors to the Jeep and placed his arm around her shoulders. "You bet."

Two hours later, Matt was maneuvering the Jeep around the hairpin curves that would take them home. He squeezed Cynthia's hand. "I can't believe how well we did! We just about paid for our whole trip."

Cynthia was sitting in the middle of the front seat, close to Matt. She grinned widely. "I had this feeling that we needed to try our luck one more time."

Matt chuckled. "Yeah, but you were pretty specific. You said the dollar machines, and you were right on!"

They had walked away with five-hundred dollars clear. Matt put his arm around her, pulling her closer to him. "I have to admit I'm getting more and more impressed with those gut feelings of yours, Honey."

She laughed. "It's about time."

Time flew, and he was soon guiding their Jeep around to the back of their apartment building. Parking it, he was amazed at how refreshed and relaxed he felt.

With their arms around each other, laughing at nothing in particular, they half-ran up the steps to their front door. He suddenly picked her up and carried her through the door, chuckling. "See! I can still do this!"

She laughed and clung to his neck. "Okay! You've proved it. Now put me down!"

He carried her over to the couch where they both fell onto the cushions, laughing. Matt leaned his head against her shoulder and said, "No cooking tonight. We're ordering pizza."

"Oh. Okay."

As he picked up the phone to order it, he heard the beeping that signified an unheard message. Pushing in his code, he was surprised to hear a message from Guy Stone, Dan Stone's father. Dan had been the first fugitive to die.

After he ordered the pizza, Matt dialed the Stone's number, and Mr. Stone answered the phone on the first ring. He seemed surprised and pleased that Matt had called back.

"Thanks for calling back, Matt. Martha and I were wondering if you and Cynthia could meet us for dinner next weekend. Either in Silverton or Durango. Whichever you prefer."

Matt replied, "I'm sure we can. Is there any particular reason you want to meet with us?"

He hesitated, then said, "We just need to talk to someone who was involved in … in the shootings. Martha and I are having a hard time understanding how Dan could have been a part of it. He was our son, and he caused so much heartache to good people."

Matt knew instantly that they were reaching out for someone to forgive *them*, which was a shame because they had not done anything wrong. Matt also knew that few people in the Four Corners area would have met with them, but that wasn't who he was.

Guy Stone was a teacher and Vietnam War Veteran who had married his childhood sweetheart. Martha ran a downtown business in Durango, and the couple had always been well-liked until the shootings.

When their son had been found dead near the river, the Stones had immediately contacted the Denver Post and expressed their deep sorrow over the murder of one officer and the wounding of others. They also sent letters of apology to each officer effected by the tragedy, including Matt and his family. The only one to respond to their heartfelt plea had been Matt.

When Matt and Cynthia met with the Stones at a downtown Durango restaurant, it was awkward at first. Mrs. Stone seemed especially nervous and tears often glistened in her eyes as she talked.

Her voice was weak and tremulous. "The autopsy was inconclusive. There are so many questions that have not been answered, and we feel like we've been left in the dark. We do *not* believe Dan killed himself! The coroner wrote that Dan's jaw was broken and there was a large imprint on his face. We can't prove it, of course, but we believe Dan may have changed his mind. Maybe he was going to turn himself in. We also think Jay Vista is the one who killed him."

Guy Stone continued, "When we heard that our son had joined up with that militia group near Delores, we were shocked. But we didn't know about it until *after* the shooting. I guess Dan had talked to his older brother, Bob, who used to be a cop. He told Bob that the government was going to take everyone's guns away and the world was going to end soon. Something about all the computers in the world going berserk. The rest he kept a secret from all of us. It's been a nightmare."

Mrs. Stone added, "Toward the end, we didn't even know where he was living or who his friends were. I wish now we'd tried harder, but we didn't want to force ourselves on him. We wanted him to stand on his own two feet, but this …." Tears welled up in her eyes once more. "We couldn't have imagined this in a hundred years."

Guy told them of how people they knew in the Cortez area shunned them after the news broke. Finally Mrs. Stone dabbed at her eyes and said, "We are so sorry that our son's actions had a part in causing your injuries. I hope you can someday forgive us."

Matt shook his head. "You weren't the one out there pulling the trigger. No one should hold you personally responsible, but I can't say I'm surprised. Some people around the Cortez area seem to like making judgments they have no business making."

Guy Stone looked at Matt. "We read about all your problems with the sheriff's office."

Matt shrugged his shoulders. "It's over now. I'm doing what I love and that part of my life is done with. As for your son, he's gone and you shouldn't feel guilty over something he chose to do. I don't blame you. It's a hazard of the job and I survived. You need to survive too."

As they were lying in bed that night, Cynthia said, "That author Tony Hillerman has written a lot about the evil that hangs around the canyonlands to the south of Cortez. One of his books even touched on the manhunt here, remember?"

"Yeah. There's always been a lot of superstition and myths in that area, but part of the problem seems to be the people who have been there a long time. The fact that they're blaming the Stones for what their son did shows they have their own twisted sense of justice. It doesn't make sense."

"So the three families have been found guilty along with their sons?"

"Sure sounds like it. Look at how some of those same people treated us. I was branded a traitor and treated like scum. The facts didn't seem to matter."

Cynthia shuddered. "I feel better up here in the mountains. All those stories about the spirits seeking revenge … that always bothered me more than I let on."

106

Matt pulled her over next to him. "That part of our life is behind us now, Cynthia. Okay?"

She nodded, but her eyes still held a question.

TWENTY-FOUR

December 1999

• • • • • • • • • • • • • • • • • • • •

Matt's second winter as a State Trooper began without any major incidents. By December, Matt was becoming more of a pro while coping with icy road conditions and danger from avalanches. During certain snowstorms, winds would often reach eighty-miles-an-hour and batter the forests like gigantic waves, causing enormous snowdrifts. He would usually be in the middle of the storm, setting up road blocks to stop traffic from proceeding further up the mountain. As expected, the worst weather usually occurred on top of Red Mountain.

He was on call whenever the snow plows were out sweeping the roads in each direction up on the passes. On one particular night, tons of debris came crashing down onto the road next to Mineral Creek. He was just coming around the especially narrow hairpin curve when a deafening noise caused him to let up on the gas pedal. He saw that the entire road was now blocked with rocks and heavy snow and a mammoth pine tree that had been pulled out by the roots. Hitting the brakes hard, he barely managed to stop the cruiser in time to avoid going over the edge of the cliff.

As Cynthia was listening to Matt's account of his narrow escape that day, she was biting her tongue. *Just listen. Don't show your fear.* This is just all a part of his job. She had accepted the dangers when she agreed to marry him.

Winter in the mountains could be grueling, but she rarely heard him complain. She kept herself busy in her coffee shop, adding new books whenever something looked interesting and had to do with the area. However, the mountain passes were often closed down during the cold winter months. The trains were no longer coming up to Silverton, and few people liked to chance the passes.

Even the locals were ensconced in their warm homes, huddling around wood stoves and preferring not to brave the weather unless totally necessary.

Still, people in the downtown area would come in for coffee and a cinnamon roll just to talk. It did get lonesome when few visitors ventured up.

This particular evening was bitter cold out, and they had a fire blazing in the wood stove. She had moved the small sofa close to the stove so they could sit cuddled under blankets and talk over their day.

Leaning her head against Matt's shoulder, she responded to his near accident. "Your guardian angel is still hanging around, Honey. Thank God."

He chuckled and took a sip of the hot coffee she had just brewed. "Yep. So, how was your day?"

"Slow. I had one tourist who couldn't believe he had arrived alive." She laughed. "I hope he decided to spend the night, because he didn't act very knowledgeable about driving on mountain roads with ice and snow."

"I hope you encouraged him to take a room for the night."

"I did. It was weird, but he actually asked about the shooting. Wanted to know if they had ever caught that last fugitive."

Matt raised his eyebrow. "You're kidding! Someone up here in the middle of winter, and he's asking about that?"

"I know. Maybe he was a reporter. He asked a lot of questions."

"Like what?"

"Like was Vista part of a militia group. And was that the group up here in the mountains. I told him I had no idea what Vista was doing or if he was even alive. Then I told him I hope he's dead."

Matt slowly nodded. "Hmm. Did you get his name?"

"I asked him where he was from, and he just said over in Utah, near the border. But who knows?"

"What was he driving?"

"A big four-wheel drive Durango or something like that."

"I'll check around in the morning and see if I can find out where he stayed."

When he drove off that morning, chains on his cruiser, he checked around at several motels and inns but didn't see any car matching the description Cynthia had given him. It was odd. It might have been a reporter, but nothing was going on that he knew about. Storing it in the back of his mind, he headed out of town and onto the highway.

* * *

Christmas was almost upon them when Matt found himself contending with a very different kind of problem; one called Y2K. Notices had been sent out to all law enforcement agencies in the country stating that computers around the world might shut down when they rolled over to 2000, unable to cope with the three zeroes in the new year.

Everyone in his department was being placed on full alert for the coming New Year's Eve. If any problems were going to present themselves, they would occur when the clock struck midnight, welcoming in the New Year. If a worldwide malfunctioning of computer systems did occur, it would effect Colorado considerably.

The greatest danger might come from off-and-on switches that controlled the world's nuclear bombs. There was real concern that bombs could be dispatched accidentally, destroying a good portion of the world.

Locally, lights could go out all over Colorado, including stoplights on major roads. That's where Matt would be if it should happen. He really didn't believe anything that drastic would occur, yet he would be taking all the precautions his sergeant had told him to.

When he discussed this new concern with Cynthia, she didn't feel anything catastrophic would happen either, but she decided she would stock up on groceries and water just to be on the safe side. He explained how the government had been quietly working on this problem for over three years now, which made her feel more secure.

She nodded. "Okay. Then they should have everything figured out before the deadline, right?"

"Should. I think their biggest worry will be small countries around the world who have a few bombs and little computer savvy."

"I still think it'll all be okay."

On December 30th, one day before New Year's Eve, television reporters were filming people as they prepared for the worst possible scenarios. In Silverton, generators and survival gear were being grabbed up from every store in the vicinity.

A few men who were sympathetic to some of the causes of the local militia group in Cortez began talking about the remaining fugitive, Jay Vista. One such man mentioned his thoughts to a neighbor, who in turn told his friend … a trooper in the Highway Patrol.

As the trooper listened to his friend, he felt a bit nervous. Was it true that Vista was still in the area and *had* joined up with that militia group in Silverton? And what the hell did they mean by saying they had secret plans for a takeover of Silverton on New Year's Eve?

When he asked his friend this, the man replied, "Hey, that group believes that all the world's computers are gonna' shut down at midnight, and the end of the world as we know it will come to an end. Then they … the "true patriots" … will take over the government. This guy says militia groups in every state have been stockpiling weapons for years preparing for this. And that taking hostages in Silverton will be the beginning of their role in it. They're all crazy enough to try it."

The trooper thanked his friend for the information, then told his supervisor in Durango. That supervisor contacted his headquarters in Denver and plans were put into motion to prevent such an act.

The rumor most prevalent since the heist of the water truck back in 1998 was the purpose of the theft. Apparently, the trio who stole it had planned on filling the truck with gasoline and blowing up the Hoover Dam, long a major target for terrorists.

Now, as the New Year of 2000 approached, law enforcement officials in the Four Corners area were wondering if Jay Vista really had hooked up with the militia in Silverton. Had he joined them and were they planning something as serious as the takeover of Silverton?

Matt was called into the Durango office and warned that if anything did go down at midnight, he could be a target of the group. He listened, then shook his head. "I don't think they're going to do anything. Thanks for the warning, but if something does go down, I'll be out there doing my best to stop them just like I did before."

His supervisor nodded. "I know. But you won't be alone this time."

* * *

On December 30, Sergeant Greg Watson was standing in the doorway to his office when Matt drove onto the parking lot. He motioned for Matt to join him and waited while Matt locked up his cruiser. Smiling, he said, "Come on in my office for a couple of minutes, Matt. We need to talk."

Curious, Matt followed his supervisor into the comfortable office surrounded by pictures of Greg's family. "What's up, Greg?"

"Sit down. Make yourself comfortable."

Matt did, then waited for him to begin, sensing he was more tense than usual. What he said was surprising. "Matt, we've been hearin' more rumors and you need to know about them."

"Okay."

"You're aware of the militia group near Silverton."

"Yeah."

"And you've been told that this group might try something tomorrow night, especially if you lose electricity up there. It seems they want to set off some bombs in Silverton and maybe take a few hostages."

Matt was taken aback. "What's the matter with those guys? I mean … I'm all for anyone having the right to bear arms to protect themselves. But those guys … hell, this is a group of fanatics who just want to shoot anybody they feel is inferior to them."

Greg shrugged his shoulders. "The people who tend to join these groups often come from a screwed up childhood of some kind. They feel life's given them a raw deal and they're looking for someone or something to get back at."

Matt nodded. "Yeah, or they don't want to pay their taxes. Like the guy who isolated himself up in the mountains for years and ended up leading a pretty wealthy lifestyle. When the Feds arrested him for not paying taxes for the last twenty years, he yelled about his rights being violated. What about the rights of the taxpayers who had been unknowingly supporting this guy? He's not above the law just because he calls himself a patriot."

"I agree. I guess this Y2K thing has got them all excited. Anyway, watch your back for the next twenty-four hours. Everyone's been put on alert as of today."

"Okay. I know it's been kind of hard to pin these guys down, especially when the ivy-league guy next door may be a hard-core survivalist. You don't always know who the enemy really is."

"Yeah, you got that right.. Oh … and those rumors about Jay Vista being involved with the Silverton militia have made other militia groups real happy."

Matt nodded. "Sure, because they like all the media fuss. You know … they're getting some action at last. But I don't think they planned on hundreds of cops descending on the Four Corners area and using Black

Hawk helicopters and the latest in tracking devices to go after them last year. Hopefully, it made them step back and reevaluate things."

Greg replied, "You'd think so. But if Vista is still out there … hell, he's been on the run for two years, hiding like a scared rabbit under rocks and in holes. He's a cop killer. Even if someone's helping him, how good can his life be?"

"I guess it depends on how much help he's getting. Or maybe it's all just a rumor. Maybe he's as dead as his buddies."

"I admit I wouldn't mind finding his body out there someday. But if he *is* somewhere around here, I'd like a chance at him. You know, Matt … *you* survived all they could throw at you and then you became sort of a celebrity around Colorado. You overcame your wounds and went on to the Academy. Against all the odds, you finished first in your class. Now you're supposedly livin' the good life and your wife has a successful business. It's not sittin' well with these guys."

Matt was surprised. "It wasn't personal between them and me. I was just doing my job."

"I know that. Most people know that. But just in case even one of these rumors is true, I want you wearin' your vest full time and watchin' your back. Especially if you're called out tomorrow night. We've contacted the FBI and made them aware of the rumors. If we do experience any blackouts tonight, we need to prepare for the worst."

Matt digested his words and nodded. "Okay. I understand."

"I honestly don't think anything will happen, but we'll be ready if it does. One more thing … the Four Corners militia group is rumored to be connected with one of the most extreme right-wing militias in the country. Understand?"

"Yeah. Watch my back."

As Matt drove home that evening, he was filled with conflicting emotions. He waited until after dinner to break the news to Cynthia about these new rumors. She was instantly worried. "I always knew it was that group who helped Vista! What are you going to do?"

"I'm on call for tomorrow night and if they need me, I'll go and do my job."

"Vista and his buddies nearly killed you and, like Greg said, you survived the worst they could throw at you. Maybe they want to finish the job."

"I know that worries you, but I'm prepared and that's all I can do."

She took a deep breath. "If you have to go, you'd better come back safe because I'll be waiting to have my own New Year's Eve celebration with you. Don't you disappoint me, Mister."

He grinned. "I won't."

* * *

The next evening, New Year's Eve 1999, Matt kissed Cynthia for a long moment before he left, then walked out to his cruiser. He had been called out as a precaution and was ready for whatever the night might bring. Actually, he was quietly hoping Vista *would* make an appearance tonight. Then they could put an end to the whole damned thing once and for all.

Midnight came and went without a hitch. No blackouts, no bombs exploding, no terrorist attacks and no militia takeovers. The world's computers rolled over to the Year 2000 and life went on. The militia groups went back to their secret lives and the sun came up on New Year's Day 2000.

Matt went home at dawn, quietly had a New Year's drink with Cynthia, then went to bed and slept until noon.

TWENTY-SIX

Twenty-three months after the shooting

··

When spring 2000 arrived in the high country, it seemed to rush in. Trees that had been barren and clean from their leaves all winter were now sprouting tiny green buds. They had survived the deadly cold. Snow in the mountains began melting in haste and the runoff was causing flooding down below. Rivers and creeks were swollen and some were overflowing their banks. Local rafting companies down in Durango were reveling about the crowds of people who were coming from everywhere to experience rafting at its wildest.

Matt hoped there wouldn't be any drownings as in years past. In their exuberant rush to get out on the river, people got careless despite all the warnings. If someone was thrown off the raft, he would have no idea of how easy it would be to lose his balance on the slippery, moss-covered rocks lying just below the surface of the water.

Once out of the raft, the current could suck him down and bounce him against the rocks and logs that are scattered along the bed of the river. Life jackets can protect a person only so much, and if the current is too strong, he could get caught on a submerged log or jagged rock and drown before anyone gets to him. Matt prayed this would be a year where prudence was practiced and there would be no tragedies.

Over the last few months, Cynthia's coffee shop had evolved into a huge success, and she had expanded it to twice its original size in order to sell books and gifts along with her special coffee. Also, she was talking about organizing a counseling service to aid law enforcement families who were going through what her family had experienced.

She was quite resolute in her ideas about starting such a group there in the Four Corners area. When law enforcement administrators and local county or city council members failed to give needed support to the families, they were left feeling abandoned. She had found it unforgivable the way Matt had not only been ignored while fighting to live, but had also been viciously attacked by the sheriff's office.

Matt was supportive of her efforts and wanted to do whatever he could to help implement her plans. In the meantime, as he continued covering the boundaries of his post, his thoughts rarely turned to his former employment with the sheriff's office. Yet he concurred with Cynthia that something needed to be done when such difficult situations arose, and his wife just might be the one to accomplish it.

He and Cynthia had now been married four years, which put them past the honeymoon stage, but they were still solid with each other. She had taken care of him when he had been so incapacitated, and that meant more to him than she would ever know. He didn't feel he could ever repay her for what she did. It was his belief that you needed to look at who was there for you during both the good and the bad times.

He knew his injuries, combined with age, would someday mean the end of his career in law enforcement. In the meantime he was biding his time, happy to be working at the job he loved the most. After an especially long, strenuous day, he sometimes found himself limping from pain that often felt like grinding rocks in his leg, but he just kept going. His doctors had warned him that he may be facing another operation on his knee in the future. For now though, whenever the bullet fragments caused pain, he would just bear it. He was well aware of how close he had come to a forced retirement and would be forever thankful he had been given a second chance by the State Patrol.

He and Cynthia both worked out in a home gym they had put together in their apartment. It helped keep him in shape, and she had never looked better. They enjoyed living in Silverton and had found the people there to be filled with pride for their rugged little town. Everyone seemed to enjoy sharing their experiences and stories with those who showed a genuine interest in what they were saying. Cynthia's coffee shop had become a favorite hangout for locals and tourists alike.

When their house down in Delores finally sold, they immediately put a down payment on a large Victorian house in town that they had had their eye on. It needed fixing up, but that was something Matt loved to do. He was pretty adept when working with wood and took pleasure in creating furniture and shelving. He had often considered taking it up full time when he retired.

Even though Cynthia was a flat-lander from Texas, moving to Colorado and meeting Matt had aroused her interest in high country hiking. The first time Matt had suggested she join him and a neighbor for a hike above Silverton, she was hooked.

She found herself hanging onto rock ledges, standing on her tiptoes to reach the next ledge and constantly praying for her life. She loved it! They now made hiking a regular activity they did together and had started going over to Ouray to soak in the natural hot springs after each hike.

Every spring, the town of Silverton would put on their own stage adaptation of a Broadway play, and this year they had selected "Steel Magnolias." Cynthia had been approached to play the Dolly Parton role in the play, but she was hesitant. When she was younger, she had been a cheerleader and beauty pageant contestant, but she had never tried acting in her life. Matt thought it was a great idea, and with his encouragement, she decided why not?

Weeks of learning pages and pages of dialogue, then more weeks of long rehearsal hours soon make her question why she had said yes. She had to hire extra help to run the coffee shop while she prepared for the play. Her biggest supporter, Matt, also helped keep the shop going.

When opening night arrived, her husband, family and friends were all sitting in front row seats. She was nervous, but very determined to get through it without blowing any lines, and she did! The next day, she was astonished to read such good reviews of the play in the local papers. They stated she had her southern drawl down perfectly, (easy for a Texas girl) and they applauded her comedic talents.

She was very pleased, yet surprised. She thought the reviewers would be kind to her because it was her first attempt at acting, but they really seemed impressed with her acting skills!

She and Matt read the reviews together, and he grabbed her, hugging her tightly and shouted, "My wife, the Star! We need to celebrate!"

Together they made the decision to take the following weekend to visit a favorite spot of theirs. Located near Farmington, New Mexico, just one hour southeast of Durango, they had discovered one of the most unique bed-and-breakfasts in the United States.

Named Kokopelli's Cave, it is just that. Blasted out of a 65-million-year-old sandstone cliff, the cave has everything a person could desire. Plush carpeting, soft furniture, a fully-equipped kitchen and in Matt's mind, the best of all —- a waterfall shower of hot water that flows down over flagstone rocks.

Matt knew he was now strong enough to maneuver the 185 steps leading from the top of the cliff to the entrance of the cave down below. The following Friday, Cynthia quickly packed for their long weekend and they were soon driving toward Farmington. When she spotted the turn that would take them down a narrow mountain road through thick pine trees and weird rock formations to the cave, she said, "I'm so glad we thought of this, Honey. It'll be fun."

He reached over and gently squeezed her hand. "It'll be private, that's for sure."

They arrived at the owner's ranch where they paid him for the next two days. He then jumped in his Bronco and led them to the plateau above the cave where guests park. As Matt parked the Jeep, the owner waved and took off back down the road.

They knew from staying here before that once he guided you to the parking area, you were on your own. They had to carry their own bags down the 185 steps to the cave's entrance. The real fun part is holding your luggage above your head to get through a narrow crevice with little space to squeeze your body through, let alone your baggage.

Having become a rock-climbing fanatic, Cynthia thought it was all great fun. Once they reached the front door — an actual glass sliding door — they entered into the realm of the luxurious underground cave. It boasted 1,650 feet of living space; a living room, dining room, kitchen and amazingly, a circular wall of flagstones decorated with candles.

Cynthia walked over to the center of this circular wall and looked down on a small portal in the middle of the floor and discovered a kiva: one like those found in the Anasazi ruins at Mesa Verde. She smiled at Matt. "Honey, get me a match so I can light these candles."

He grinned, "You getting a bit spooked?"

"No! I just want to be on the good side of whoever may still be here, okay?"

He chuckled and handed her some matches, then bent down to help her light them, saying, "At least they'll add the right kind of atmosphere for what I have in mind."

She raised her eyebrow. "Yeah? And what's that?"

He smiled and took her hand. "I've been thinking about that waterfall shower and the Jacuzzi all day."

She blew out the remaining match and met his eyes. "Too much thinking can be stressful. Maybe we should try it out now."

She led him away from the candles and toward the sound of running water. He began pulling his shirt over his head as they walked.

Later, they sat out on the balcony carved into the side of the cliff and watched as the sun went down in a maze of colors. The distant San Juan Mountains faded into darkness, and the sounds of the high desert country became louder with the night. As the evening air grew crisp and cold, they decided to go inside and shut out the desert sounds for the complete silence of the cave.

Matt chose a Native American flute CD to play while Cynthia went through the cupboards and refrigerator to see what was available to cook for their dinner. Along with the fully-stocked kitchen, the owner had installed a state-of-the-art entertainment center including a 35-inch plasma television set and DVD player.

After fixing a light dinner of broiled steak, bread and a salad, they retired to the living room to watch a couple of videos. Eventually they began getting sleepy, so they wandered into the master bedroom with its queen platform bed. Pulling back the soft down quilts and fresh-smelling sheets, they climbed up onto the bed where they soon fell asleep listening to the sound of falling water coming from the rock shower.

The next day Cynthia wanted to shop in Aztec, a small town with lots of Victorian buildings and great little shops at the Aztec Museum and Pioneer Village. She ended up buying a Native American sand painting while Matt found a pair of hand-tooled cowboy boots. Later that night, they returned to their cave retreat.

The Kokopelli is the flute player of Navajo legends, and he is said to represent joy and happiness. It seemed an appropriate name for this uncommon earthen cave that had been made into what felt like a safe retreat from the busy world outside … something Matt was learning to appreciate more and more.

Later, as Matt lie listening to his wife's soft breathing next to him, he stared at the candles still glowing in the darkness and could not imagine how his life would be if he could no longer climb those 185 steps or hike the mountain trails by Silverton. He knew his leg may let him down someday, but with luck and God's help, it wouldn't happen until he was ready to retire.

Even then, he'd keep going with either an artificial knee or whatever they could do to help him. He had fought and conquered devastating pain, and he could certainly get through another operation if it would keep him on his feet.

Smiling to himself, he rolled over and placed his arm around Cynthia's waist, feeling her stir and cuddle closer to him. He loved her spunk and fighting spirit, and most of all, her loyalty. This was one marriage that was going to make it.

TWENTY-FIVE

Every now and then, Matt would find himself crossing paths with some of the deputies from his old department. They never acknowledged his presence, even if they ended up in the same restaurant or coffee shop. He was aware that Sanchez was still annoyed at him, but it didn't bother him any. None of those people were a part of his life now, and they were rarely in his thoughts. He had recently heard rumors that it was anything but peaceful back at his old department, with lots of disagreements between Sanchez, Catlin and others. In his opinion, they all deserved each other.

One evening he came home from work with a mischievous grin on his face. Cynthia looked at him and knew something was up. "You look like the cat who just swallowed the canary. What's that big ol' grin about?"

He took off his gun and hat and sat down at the kitchen table. Looking up at her, he said, "What I heard today doesn't exactly surprise me, but damn, I'm kind of enjoying it."

"What?"

"That whole fiasco with Sheriff Catlin … giving my promotion to Sanchez in order to force me out. Remember all the promises Sanchez made to Catlin?"

"Of course I do. And Sanchez got Catlin the job he asked for."

"Yeah, he did. And today Sanchez *fired* him."

Cynthia gasped. "You're kidding!"

Matt chuckled. "It did me good when I heard that. All of Catlin's big plans have gone down the toilet. Such a nice guy, too."

Cynthia started laughing. "I can't believe it! After all he put you through … all that crap about how the *best* man won. I wonder what he thinks of Sanchez now?"

"You know what? He lied and tried to discredit me and it's all come back to bite him." Matt's eyes were twinkling as he looked at her.

She got up and headed toward the kitchen. "This calls for a celebration!"

She came back carrying two wine glasses and an unopened bottle of Merlot. He helped take the cork out and poured the wine into the glasses.

Toasting her, he said, "To Catlin and Sanchez … it couldn't happen to more likable guys."

If wasn't long before he heard that one deputy after another was quitting to go to other law enforcement agencies. It seemed crime was on the rise in sleepy little Cortez and people were getting hurt and even killed. One guy shot his girlfriend in the face, and a fellow State Trooper was shot four times while patrolling near the Indian casino outside Cortez.

When that happened, a reporter from the Denver Post phoned Matt and asked for a phone interview. When Matt consented, he began by comparing this latest shooting in the Four Corner area to the 1998 shootings and huge manhunt in which Matt was a casualty.

The wounded trooper, a canine handler, had stopped a speeding car in a routine traffic stop. Just like in 1998, the suspect came out shooting, then disappeared into the canyonlands. However, this suspect did not escape. A tribal policeman on the Ute Mountain Reservation had recognized the car and approached it, gun ready. The suspect suddenly shot himself in the chest, but had since recovered. He was now facing first degree attempted murder charges against a peace officer. The wounded trooper recovered.

When Matt was asked if he ever worries about Jay Vista still being free, he replied. "No. My wife worries that the past might catch up to me someday, but it hasn't so far. No, I don't worry."

Matt knew that each year the Cortez Police Department held a memorial service for the officer who was killed by the three fugitives in 1998. He still appreciates the Cortez Police Department for taking him under their wings after the sheriff's office pushed him out the door.

He also knows that a cop today has to protect the public, watch his own back, protect the rights of criminals and, even if a suspect is holding a weapon, he can't shoot unless he has proof the perp will use that weapon. It isn't as simple as it used to be.

TWENTY-SIX

Matt encountered his first near-fatal accident of the season in May of that year. An eighty-year-old man had lost control of his car and it slid sideways over the edge of a hairpin curve on the way to Silverton. His seventy-nine-year-old wife was the only passenger. Miraculously, the car had landed on a small ledge, preventing them from falling thousands of feet. It took the Jaws of Life to extract the couple from the car, yet they only received minor cuts and bruises from their terrifying ride straight down the side of the mountain. When he had first looked over the edge to see the crushed car far below, he thought they would be dead.

To see them live to tell their story was what made his job so rewarding.

That same day, Cynthia was getting ready to go to the coffee shop and was pleased to find that the weather was turning warmer. She loved summer in the mountains and this last winter had been too long and too cold. She was tired of the snow and ice and had been longing for warmer weather. Today was actually pleasant and the breeze blowing up from the canyons felt warm.

As she glanced through the open window, she spotted the first of the tiny mountain flowers that would soon be breaking through the snow everywhere once the sun melted it down to a thin layer. Down in Durango everything was beginning to bloom, but up here at 10,000 feet, she was thrilled to see even one flower. Happy at her find, she went back to the task of getting dressed for work.

Everyone in town seemed to be noticing the changes in the weather too, and her coffee shop was exceptionally busy that day. She had hired a lady named Belle to help out part-time and was thankful for her aid today. Once the rush was over, she told Belle that she was going to take a short break to read one of the small newspapers distributed by local publishers.

Her peaceful morning quickly changed in the second it took her to look at the headlines. Shock rushed through her! *No! How could John, the Editor of the paper, print such garbage?*

It was written under the guise of a "found letter" to a mother and was a thinly disguised account of the flight of the last fugitive, Jay Vista. Using the pseudonym of 'Jack,' it told of his 'hardships' since he had been running from the law.

'Jack' told of holding his gun to his own mouth, but of not being able to pull the trigger. He wrote that he buried his guns under a pile of rocks, but he didn't explain why. *Could it be he was hiding the gun that he used to shoot both of his buddies with?*

Then he compared shooting a cop to taking a long drink of cold Dr. Pepper; that it hurt at first, but then it felt good. 'Jack' talked of missing his mother and the 'green grass of home' … words taken directly from a country song of many years ago.

Cynthia's emotions were still raw beneath the surface and this article brought everything rushing back. Her first thoughts were that someone had given this letter to John, hoping he would print it —- someone who had direct contact with Jay Vista.

She had always felt in her heart that Vista was still alive. By John agreeing to print such an article, he was making public the callous and cruel thoughts of a killer who had nearly ended her husband's life. The fact that he printed this piece of crap to sell newspapers was, in her eyes, a very low and heartless thing to do.

Jay Vista and his buddies had begun a killing spree in which they killed one cop, seriously wounded several others and left her husband for dead. So what if this monster had to contend with *gnats and heat* while hiding from the law? If this letter was meant to conjure up sympathy for the "poor man who misses his mother," all it did was remind Cynthia of the kind of evil Vista represented.

As she re-read the part where he had supposedly put a gun to his own head but couldn't pull the trigger, her hands felt shaky and all she could think of was how much she wished he had been less a coward. It would have ended that part of the anguish and pain he had caused so many people; people who were the *REAL* victims.

Suddenly the mountains surrounding Silverton appeared ominous to her. They seemed to be leaning closer to her, daring her to look at their unseen secrets. The day was overcast, and the clouds were hovering over the town, obscuring the road leading up toward the mountain peaks.

She put the paper down and stared out the front window of her coffee shop. The colorful boardwalks and Victorian architecture of the town now looked slightly out of focus. Conflicting emotions raged inside her, causing scared as well as angry feelings to rise up in her. Shouldn't this be over with? It had been two years since the shooting, and now this letter shows up in one of the local newspapers!

Her thoughts flew back to the day she had spotted that man dressed in camouflage standing in her yard, staring at her through the front window. She sensed Matt still didn't believe it had been Vista. Yet she was just as sure it was. The killer was arrogantly letting Matt know he was still around and knew where they lived.

Jay Vista and his cohorts hadn't cared about the aftermath of pain and anguish they left behind following their 'run for fun.' A run they had sat down and planned out; one they had decided they would not come back from. They hadn't considered the wives and children who were left to deal with dead or critically-wounded fathers and husbands just because these three guys decided to not only run, but also to kill as they ran.

When Matt returned home that evening, she showed him the newspaper and waited until he had read it all. When he put the paper down, his voice was gentle as he spoke. "These are just words, Honey. They mean nothing. Even if Vista is still around here, it's not about us."

"It *is* about us!" Her voice rose in volume. "I'm still so angry at what those men did to *you*. Our whole life changed that day. You're *still* suffering from your injuries. How can it *not* be about us, Matt? How can it not be?"

He stared at her for a long moment, startled at her burst of emotion. "I didn't know it still affected you this much."

Tears came to her eyes. "Well, of course it does!"

To her dismay, more tears began rolling down her cheeks and she couldn't stop them. Matt held her tightly as she sobbed in broken gasps, letting all her hurts and fears force themselves to the surface. Tears came unbidden to Matt's eyes as he realized she had been holding so much back for a long time.

He stood there holding her until she started to calm down, and then he gently guided her over to the couch. Sitting down with her, he took her hands in his and looked into her eyes. "Honey, I am so sorry that you've been carrying around these feelings all by yourself. Can I tell you what I think?"

She nodded silently, her breathing still sounding ragged. "Okay. I know it's rumored Vista's still out there and this letter just conjures everything up again. Personally, I think he's either dead or he's a hell of a long way from here. He doesn't want to be caught and to come back here would be risking too much."

Cynthia met his eyes. "But he's arrogant, Matt. He wants you and the world to know he's still free. This article is Vista thumbing his nose at every cop in Colorado. And John was wrong to print it."

TWENTY-SEVEN

Matt knew that being in law enforcement was not easy on his family and nearly being killed had made it that much worse. Cynthia was strong and he was confident she would soon gather her strength and rise above this latest setback. Anger boiled in him and he felt like confronting John, even though he knew reporters wrote what they thought would sell newspapers. It wasn't anything he could arrest the guy for.

If Vista *was* being hidden by one of the local militia groups, he wanted him caught. It would end the speculation and then Cynthia could put it to rest once and for all. Or maybe Vista's new buddies would take him out themselves, and he'd get another phone call one of these days saying a third body had been found deep in the canyonlands.

Survivalist or not, the odds were against anyone out there. Between the heat of the summer and the cold of the winter, there wasn't a lot of comfort in the canyonlands. There was either too little water or there was flooding, with wild animals just as hungry as you might be. If Vista was still alive, someone was helping him, probably out of a misplaced sense of sympathy for his 'cause' —- whatever that cause was.

Hometown boys can go bad just like anyone else. He still felt sorrow whenever he thought about what the parents of the three fugitives must be going through, knowing their sons were killers. He, of all people, knew the world wasn't a perfect place. His job was to try and make things safer for the public, but no one could ever have predicted something like the Four Corners tragedy. On a larger scale, who could have predicted the Oklahoma bombing?

He had been amazed and proud of the bravery he saw then, when policemen, firemen and ordinary citizens in Oklahoma had gone into Ground Zero to try and help. So many had lost their lives during that catastrophe, including small children.

In a tiny, remote corner of Colorado, a white water truck had been stolen for unknown reasons. When the officer who had been killed pulled that truck over, had he prevented something as extreme as the demolition of the Hoover Dam? That was still the big rumor floating around.

Matt used to relive the shooting many times in his mind, feeling the bullets hitting him and fearing he would never see his family again. Those moments would always be with him, but they had also made him a stronger and more perceptive law officer.

Now, he is one trooper in a large stretch of wilderness who stands between the public and those who would break the law. As a Highway Patrolman, he is there to protect the roads so people can travel in peace and experience the beauty of the mountains that he sees every day. Maybe the day will come when he and Jay Vista will face each other again. Maybe not.

Either way, he loves what he is doing. If people like those in the local militia groups consider him and his fellow officers the enemy, so be it. As long as they comply with the law, he won't have a problem with them.

He also knows he will never, ever bow down to people like Catlin and Sanchez. Whether you are a militant who uses violence to bend people to your way of thinking, or you are a county sheriff who uses your power to get people to do your bidding, it's basically the same. It's not American.

Tomorrow was Saturday, and he, Cynthia and his son, Josh, were heading for the mountains once more. It had been almost two years before he was finally able to take his family on that camping trip promised back in 1998.

They had traded in their tent for a small, enclosed camper when he found the ground was too uncomfortable for his leg and arm. He had bought Josh a brand new pup tent because his son was turning into a chip-off-the-old-block. Josh liked everything wild and natural and was becoming a better camper than his father.

Cynthia had been having some recent health problems with her legs, but was mending rapidly. He had found himself as the caregiver for her after the doctors operated to remove several noncancerous tumors from the calf of her leg.

He had helped run the coffee shop, cared for her and still went to work five days a week. It was hard, but she had done it for him. They are both survivors and Matt hopes that whoever reads his story will understand that seemingly impossible odds *can* be overcome.

Helen Keller once wrote, "Stay on the path of integrity, and you'll never get lost."

To do so takes perseverance and faith. If you're lucky, you'll have the love of family and friends to get you through it. He and Cynthia also had their faith in God to carry them through the worst of it. Evil had reached out for him that day in May, but a miracle had occured. No, he had not escaped unscathed, but he had managed to overcome his wounds and move on. Life is rarely easy, but he had made it. He was a survivor.

EPILOGUE

2003 ... five years after the shooting.

....

The Anasazi Indians — the Ancient Ones — are quiet. No sightings of the ghosts of Butch Cassidy or the Ute Indian princess, Chipeta, have been reported. Even the primitive, mysterious sunbaked mesas of southwestern Colorado are pervaded by serenity.

A plane rolls into the Cortez airport, and a tall, thin man with short-cropped hair, dark glasses and a mustache leans over to smile at the young boy sitting between him and a woman the man assumes is the boy's mother. "I told you it wouldn't take long to get here from Albuquerque."

The boy had told the man he was ten-years-old. "Yeah, I guess you're right, Mister."

"Don't forget to visit the One-Hundred-Year-Old Mine. You might find some gold down there if you're lucky."

The mother looks at the stranger curiously. "Did you know there was a big manhunt here a few years ago? And they never caught that last killer."

The tall man's face changes ever-so-slightly. "That's what I hear."

His tone startles her, and she finds herself looking into eyes that send a deep chill through her. She turns to her son. "Okay, honey, we need to go now. Excuse us, Sir."

She and the boy stand up and quickly push past him, gathering their bags as they go. The man remains in his seat until most of the plane has emptied. Only then does he take his duffel bag down from the overhead cabinet. Politely thanking the airplane's crew, he bypasses the baggage claim area because he is traveling light.

Slowly walking outside into the warm, dry air of the high desert country, he pauses to take a long, deep breath. A slight wind is kicking up dust along a sidewalk leading to the parked cars. Looking out at the rugged hills rising up through the haze, he smiles.

Everything that put those cops at a disadvantage worked to my advantage. Their dogs couldn't track me in the dust. Their helicopters with their infrared sensors didn't work because of the heat in the canyon walls.

*Everyone still talks about that cop, Nelson, and how he beat the odds. How he survived. Yeah, but it was nothin' compared to what I did. I walked right through a net of five-hundred cops, and they couldn't catch me. **I am the true survivor.***

He begins walking across the rocky ground toward a river bank adjacent to the airport. The expansiveness of the desert seems to gather him up, and he disappears into the ever-changing terrain.

THE END

AUTHORS' NOTE:

The scenario we ended the book on was a "rumor" told to us by a friend. We took all the "rumors" we had been made aware of by various people and came up with the scene portrayed here.

Jay Vista remains free today. No one has discovered his body in the canyonlands. Too many people in the Four Corners swear they have seen him or talked to him on too many occasions for it to be just a "rumor."

Cynthia remains adamant that he is still around. Matt isn't as sure, but doesn't discount all the rumors. It is a mystery that will not be settled until either Vista's remains are found or he is captured.

ABOUT THE AUTHORS

Shirlee Forteneaux, a business major, began as a freelance writer following a car accident that left her young son permanently disabled. She has written a column on the handicapped for the Phoenix Gazette and has been published in various magazines and newspapers in Colorado. Also an artist of wildlife, she and her son now reside in Prescott, Arizona.

Kathleen Quackenbush, sister of Shirlee, is a college graduate and the mother of two teenage boys. She has put her editing and proofreading skills to work, along with her love of writing, to co-write this book. Kathleen resides in Phoenix, Arizona.

Printed in the United States
19194LVS00005B/425